Crazy

(Vampire Love)

By
Eve Langlais

A crazy kind of love.
Langlais

Copyright & Disclaimer

SECOND EDITION
Copyright © October 2013, Eve Langlais
Cover Art by SelfPubBookCovers.com/Shardel©October 2013
Originally Edited (2011) by Victoria Miller
Second Edition Edited (2013) by Amanda Pederick

Produced in Canada
Published by Eve Langlais
1606 Main Street, PO Box 151, Stittsville, Ontario, Canada, K2S1A3

www.EveLanglais.com

ISBN-13: 978-1492781677

ISBN-10: 1492781673

Prologue

Do it. Ask him. We dare you, the voices in her head whispered slyly. Ella knew she shouldn't, yet the sibilant murmurs kept up their insistent and persistent verbal barrage. Still, she tried to refrain from giving in to their demands, especially since parents didn't approve of her invisible friends.

Chicken. You're afraid to ask, they taunted.

No, she wasn't. Truth told, she found herself curious as to the answer. But, what if her parents punished her again? She didn't like going to the dark place. Didn't like the prayers she had to recite on her knees on the hard floor.

I don't mean to be wicked. Surely it wasn't her fault she couldn't help hearing things no one else could? She tried to be a good girl. Truly she did, to ignore the insistent prodding, but the voices didn't like it when she didn't do as they asked. Her parents weren't the only ones who could punish. In the end, she gave in to their wishes. She always did.

"Daddy, why do you kiss the lady with the yellow hair?" she asked, as she ate her bowl of Fruit Loops.

Her father peered at her over his newspaper and frowned, a look she was more than familiar with. "What are you talking about?"

"The lady that works in your office. Why do you kiss her and take off your clothes to wrestle?"

The clattering of dishes made Ella turn her head and she saw her mother staring at her with a white face and open mouth.

"Who told you such dirty things?" her mother asked in a tight voice.

Uh-oh. Ella cringed at her expression, and wished, not for the first time, she'd kept the knowledge the voices deemed fit to impart to herself. "*They* told me. *They* say daddy's cheating, but I don't understand the game."

The crack of her mother's hand across her face didn't surprise her, but the sting brought tears to her eyes. The murmuring voices in her head quieted—too late. Her mother said not another word, her eyes spoke for her. She pointed towards the stairs and Ella bolted for her room, more specifically the closet at the back. She knew better than to disobey. Dropping to her bony knees, she clasped her hands together and prayed as the priests taught her.

"Heavenly father, I am a sinner beset by demons. I pray for your forgiveness. I pray you help me to cast out the demons who curse me. Please grant me your strength and wisdom that I might fight the wickedness in me. Amen." Again. "Heavenly father…" Over and over she recited the simple prayer, the voices in her head silent. They'd achieved their goal. Getting her into trouble.

Perhaps she was wicked as her mother told her. Maybe she did have a demon within her as their local pastor claimed. Something had to be wrong with her. Even at her tender age, she knew she wasn't like other children.

Not for the first time, she wondered why she had to suffer. As she prayed, her soft murmurs couldn't hide the back and forth screaming of her mother and father one floor below her. The crying as her parents fought-again. At seven, she didn't understand what divorce and betrayal meant, but she quickly learned. Her parents split up that same night and less than a month later, Ella clutching a ragged teddy, entered her first institution where she learned a whole bunch of new words like 'multiple personalities' and 'psychosis'. She also learned that it wasn't just her mother and father who didn't care if she cried; neither did the bevy of nurses and doctors who tried to fix her.

Alone in her room at night, the wails of others a constant echo to join the cacophony in her head, she prayed, not to cast out the demons who plagued her, but for a hug, someone to care for her. Anyone. Because even though Ella never saw her parents again, she wasn't completely alone, the voices in her head kept her company—and in trouble.

Chapter One

Years later. . .

The damned voices woke her out of a sound sleep.

"Run! He's gonna eat you."

"Evil. Evil. Evil. . ."

"Stupid girl. Move before he makes you his next victim."

A new voice also joined her regular cacophony with just one simple word repeated over and over, in a soothing tone. *"Sleep."*

Lying atop the mattress, the springs digging into her back, Ella rolled her eyes. Stupid voices. Couldn't they make up their minds? She had been sleeping, but now that they had her conscious, forget slumber. As one, they told her to look and see what frightened them. They drew her attention to a shadow that moved through the ward.

She sighed. *Great, another product of my warped mind.* Treating them like the child that called wolf, she ignored their cries to flee, because after all, this wouldn't be the first time her friends in the attic of her mind made her see things and then laughed when she reacted.

Slowly, the ghostly shape flowed from bed to bed, dipping down low and then rising again to move onto the next bed and its sleeping occupant. Ella found herself watching in fascination, ignoring the fevered pitch of the voices screaming at her to hide. *This is the most realistic hallucination I've ever experienced. Maybe I'm still sleeping.* That or she'd finally taken another dip around the bend into la-la land.

The shadow finally reached her bedside, and startled, Ella realized that she stared at someone quite real, although perhaps not human. For the first time in her twenty five years of life, the loud chatter in her head abruptly stopped, some mid sentence, and she felt oddly enough...alone. Empty. How unexpected and new.

"Sleep."

The command not spoken aloud, echoed in her currently vacant mind, but Ella had finally learned after many painful years of mistakes to ignore the commands of the voices that constantly tried to guide her. "No, thanks."

More insistently. *"Your eyes are getting heavy. Your body is tired. Heavy. Time for you to sleep."*

"Nah. I'm good." she said instead of closing her eyes.

"Why are you not obeying?" How disgruntled the apparition seemed. How realistic. Usually her voices stuck to speaking in her mind. She'd never had one manifest itself before.

"Who are you?" She cocked her head to one side in curiosity. The figure, dressed she noticed in a dark cloak that blended with the night, drew back and did not answer.

"Are you real?" Or not? With the drugs she took, who knew. Perhaps she saw her first ghost. Only one way to find out. Ella reached a hand out and her fingertips briefly touched the silky edge of the cape.

Scrambling to a seated position, her sudden motion saw the stranger step back, his cloak swirling around his legs. The darkness of the ward made the face hidden within the shadowed hood indistinct, but she drew in a sharp breath when she saw a pair of eyes flare red for a second.

"What are you?" she breathed. A part of her wondered that she didn't tremble in fright, or scream for help. Surely anything that could cow the voices that had been her companions for so long was something she should fear, yet this change in her monotonous life intrigued her. *Finally, something new.*

She found herself strangely drawn to the stranger and wished she could see his face. Discover if he were young or old. She desperately wanted to see if he was the savior she'd dreamed would one day arrive to sweep her out of a world she did not belong in. That prophecy of long ago, lived out in realistic color via a nightly dream. A promise that one day this nightmare would end, a fantasy not yet fulfilled, but hoped for. A mirage of her mind that she clung to tenaciously because it was all she had. Its vague promise was what had kept her sane for all the years of her incarceration because she'd long ago learned, she could not escape on her own.

Finally, the stranger spoke, his voice low and cutely disgruntled. "Why is it you don't sleep?"

"Why should I?" she answered back pertly.

"Because I said so."

"And do people always do as you say?"

"Yes."

"Must be nice." If only she possessed that ability then maybe she could get her loquacious friends to shut up. The refreshing silence in her head was so relaxing.

"It is nice, when they listen. Which, you are not."

"Why should I? I'm not tired."

"You should be. It's night. Humans sleep at night."

"I know. And I was until you arrived and woke me."

"I did no such thing. I was quite silent."

"Oh, it wasn't you. Well it was, but not entirely." How to explain his presence set off an alarm system in her mind? Hmm, perhaps she should keep that tidbit to herself. No need for him to think of her as crazy. Then again, he probably already assumed she was given her current residence.

"I need to leave." He swirled abruptly, and panic suffused her.

"No, please wait. Don't go." Ella hopped out of bed, the short white gown of the institution barely covering her knees. She almost collided with him when he turned back towards her.

"Foolish girl. Do you seek to die? Count yourself lucky that I am feeling merciful this eve."

Ella tilted her head and tried to read his expression, but the gloom in the ward only allowed for brief glimpses of hard planes. "Die? That's a little drastic don't you think. Just so you know, I don't intend to tell anyone about your visit."

He snorted. "Do you really think anyone would believe you if did?"

Ella smiled mischievously. "I guess not. After all I am nuts. For all I know perhaps you're not really here."

"Oh, I'm here unfortunately," he grumbled. "Why do you not fear me like a normal human should?"

"I'm not normal of course," she retorted. "Would I be here if I was?"

The chuckle took her by surprise and spread an unexpected warmth through her. "Why are you here?"

No point in lying. "I hear voices, and sometimes I see things."

"What do the voices say?"

"Actually, they shut up when you arrived. That's never happened before and I've got to say, it's kind of nice."

"Glad to be of service."

The low timbre of his voice did strange things to her tummy. It made her feel hot and tingly, pleasantly so. "Who are you and why are you here?"

"It's best you don't know."

"Best for who? We've already ascertained I'm crazy and people won't believe me."

"There's no need for introductions given we shall never see each other again."

"Why not?"

The sound of a key scraping in the lock of the door for the ward made him curse. "I must leave."

"Will you come back? Please." Ella heard the pleading tone in her voice and while it annoyed her, she knew she wanted to see him again. Had to. She couldn't explain why, only knew she didn't want to see him go.

"Probably not." With a swirl of his cape, he

melted into the shadows.

The door to the ward swung open and a bobbing flashlight shone in the room. Ella scurried back to her bed and pulled the covers over her head.

A moment later, the night nurse, who acted more like a guard, left. Ella knew the mysterious visitor had gone as well because the voices came back in a wild rush.

"He's gone. Evil creature."

"Oh hush," she told them. "I found him rather pleasant."

"Bloodsucker. Stealer of souls..." The voices went on a rant.

Sighing, Ella settled down amidst the wails and cries in her head. Used to the noise in her mind, she fell asleep, dreaming of a tall, dark stranger with an indistinct face, dreams that left her hot and strangely aching. A dream she'd almost given up on that saw her finally leaving the institution and living a normal life. A life in the real world. A world where someone gave a damn, and believed in hugs.

Chapter Two

What just happened in there? Zane stared up at the psychiatric institution in consternation. Never before had he encountered a human that could resist his beguilement. Never before had he met a mortal who intrigued him enough to engage him in conversation. In one night and in one petite, fragile bodied woman, he'd found both, plus an unexpected attraction. Ill-fitting gown or not, only a blind man would have missed the subtle feminine curves and delicate fine boned beauty of the patient who refused to lie down and let him feed.

A shame because I'll bet she tastes delicious.

His dark hunger rumbled in agreement. Damn, he could go for a bite right about now. Just not here, not when the girl could so easily resist him. He could never return here, a pity because this place had provided a perfect feeding ground, if a somewhat drugged one. The patient had to be new. He'd been using this blood buffet for years and never encountered her before, he would have remembered.

As he stalked through the shadows back to his car, which he'd left parked a few miles back so as to not arouse suspicion, he tried to erase her image from his mind. Even in the dark, with his enhanced eye sight, he'd caught every detail from her ash blonde hair hanging jaggedly below her shoulders to her rosebud mouth pursed in curiosity instead of fear. Her eyes, a blue so clear as to be almost translucent, had stared at him in fascination instead of dilating in fear. The shapeless garment that all the patients wore, had clung to her body revealing pert breasts with high, pointed nipples, rounded hips and he'd even smelled arousal. Sweet, sticky honey desire…

The blood he'd ingested rushed and converged in one location, painfully so. *Lusting for a slip of a girl. Why now after all these years? I know better than to play with my food.* Speaking of eating, he couldn't help but recall her fragrant bouquet, an aroma like no human he'd ever encountered before. Different, yet enticingly so.

Zane cursed. *Why can't I stop thinking about her?* She was a human, a mere mortal, and below his notice. She and the others of her kind served one purpose only-dinner. Although he'd bet judging by her sweet aroma, she'd be tastier than most.

Chapter Three

Legs hung over the arm rest of the chair, Ella twirled her hair with one finger. The voices in her head yacked away, but she ignored them as she thought of the man, or was he a phantom, from the previous night.

"Ella, are you listening?" Sharply spoken, her voices tittered recognizing the chastising tone.

Oops. Caught not paying attention. The staff didn't like it when she did that. Focusing on the present instead of the previous eve, she gazed upon her new doctor. She'd transferred here two days ago when her old institution had finally shut down for health reasons-AKA mold in the walls. Personally, she thought the rust in the water, the rats in the dorm rooms, and the leaky roof would have acted as early indicators that some repair was needed, but apparently it took some fuzzy black growth to really panic people. Whatever the reason, the patients got divvied up, she got shipped off to a new hospital, and life went on. Same rules, same restrictions, different faces.

Now that she focused on him, her new head shrink started over. "Hello Ella. Nice of you to join me."

"I didn't know I had a choice."

He ignored her impertinent reply. "I've been reviewing your file," said Dr. Peters, a man who appeared to be in his early thirties with already

14

receding brown hair and small round glasses. "It says you've been hearing voices all your life."

"As far back as I can remember," she confirmed, restraining a sigh. Did they always have to point out the obvious? Each new doctor was the same. First, they asked her questions they knew the answer to. Then they started a new regime of drugs—most of which would have made Jim Morrison smile vacuously. She could have told them not to bother. None of the pills had any effect on her, her attic friends wouldn't allow it, that or she'd grown resistant. They didn't like it when people tried to silence them. Only one thing, or should she say person, had managed to quiet the constant noise in her head and she had no idea if she'd ever see him again.

"And these voices, are they consistent?"

"If you're asking if they're the same ones over and over, then yes, for the most part. Some are louder than others. Every now and then a few will seem to disappear only to return at a later date."

"Do you know why they speak to you?"

"No." But she'd often wondered. An explanation for why she heard them wouldn't have cured all her problems, but at least maybe then she'd understand why she got singled out.

"Because you're special."

"Evil."

"Good."

Even the voices couldn't make up their mind as to why she heard them. Her most recent theory was aliens. Aliens had done something to her as a child and made her some kind of inter galactic voice receptor. For what purpose, she'd not yet decided, but wondering about it passed the time and irritated her attic friends to no end.

She realized the doctor still spoke and she held back a yawn. Why he insisted on a late evening visit, she'd forgotten to ask. Most doctors preferred to do their job during normal nine to five hours.

"…given the lack of success in the past, I'd like to try a new direction with your treatment. How would you feel about stopping all the meds?"

That caught her attention and she almost fell off the chair. "Excuse me?"

"I said, how would you feel about stopping your meds?"

"Awesome." Too late it occurred to her this might be some kind of trick. Usually the doctors wanted to dope her up more, not less. "Why would you do that?"

Brown eyes reflecting a concern she'd rarely seen, stared into hers. "Let's talk honestly here. The medications you've been given have not affected your hearing of the voices, am I right?"

Ella nodded.

"There's no point in you taking them then is there? I propose instead of trying to overpower the voices with drugs that instead we teach you to live with them. From what I've read, you've made good progress with that already."

"He wants something. Don't trust him." The voices seemed to agree on this unanimously. So of course, she ignored them.

"I think that sounds like an excellent idea, Dr. Peters. When do we start?"

"Right now."

A doctor who didn't waste time. How novel.

The rest of the late night session passed quickly as they discussed what the voices wanted of her and how she should respond. Easy answers—ignore, ignore, ignore. She didn't bring up, and neither did the doctor, the occasional incidents where the voices had physically manifested. Perhaps like some of the others, he didn't believe in the impossible. Those small acts of violence that she had no control over, though, were the reason time and time again, she'd found her pleas to be released ignored. What a shame that while her voices seemed capable of brewing mischief, they couldn't apply themselves to helping her escape.

But perhaps she could leave the hospital legally. Dr. Peters seemed optimistic, more so than her other physicians. Although some of the questions her doctor asked had seemed odd. Like how many voices did she hear? Were they always right in their predictions? Ella answered honestly. Lying, she'd discovered, ended up becoming too complicated after a while. Heck, she had a hard enough time keeping track of the truth, what with the constant whispering in her mind. She'd never understood why she'd even been labeled crazy in the first place. So what if she heard things no one else could, did it count for nothing that she was always right? Every prediction of the voices spot on, a pity most people couldn't handle the truth. The problem remained though, that once in the system, it became almost impossible to leave.

When her therapy session ended without her imaginary friends throwing anything—yet—and she returned to her ward, she thought upon her favorite fantasy. Leaving the hospital and going out into the real world. It amazed her that Dr. Peters seemed willing to even entertain the notion that she might learn to function well enough with the voices that she could eventually leave the hospital. The idea of leaving the confining walls of the institution both frightened and exhilarated her. *What would it be like to walk real streets? To shop and interact with people who had no psychological classifications? To fall in love...*

She couldn't help picturing her dark visitor of the previous night. *Is he the one? The one I dreamt of long ago when I first entered the sterile walls of my first asylum? The one destined to help me escape?*

She'd never told anyone about those visions. Heck, she'd pretty much forgotten them. Given up. And yet for months when she first entered the asylum, and cried herself to sleep every night, she dreamt of the dark man. He came to save her, not just from the hospital but from the madness in her mind. In his arms, she found peace, freedom...love.

Lost in her reverie, she didn't dodge the pinch of her ass cheek in time. Pretending nothing happened, because no one ever believed the crazy girl over a staff member, she couldn't admit to surprise. This type of thing was appalling common, after all, they were the abandoned ones. Left in the hands of doctors and staff by well meaning—or not—family members. Those that seemed abandoned, people like Ella who had no friends or family on the outside, were especially vulnerable. Sexual misconduct, rape, abuse, all of those things flourished with no one to complain to. No one to advocate or protect them. A pinch on the ass might seem minor in the grand scheme of things, but she knew what it meant. First it started with little things, a subtle touch here, a fondle there. Then it escalated to threats or acts of violence if a patient didn't comply, didn't give in. Ella felt sorry for those unlucky ones. But what about herself? The guard didn't frighten her. No one did. Her voices excelled at protecting her from this kind of thing.

The night orderly, not the same one from the previous nights, placed himself in front of her. He smirked and licked his lips. Ella didn't show him the shudder she felt inside. She didn't fear this overgrown bully, although he did gross her out. He was welcome to try and intimidate her. He'd learn soon enough that the voices didn't tolerate his type.

"Pig," they echoed in agreement.

But unfortunately, any action her attic friends took would probably affect Dr. Peters plan to rehabilitate her. And that really pissed her off, sending the voices in her head into a spinning frenzy that manifested in her hair floating around her head for one ghostly moment.

The fantasy was nice while it lasted though, she thought with a sigh.

Chapter Four

What am I doing? Have all those years of feeding on the insane finally caused me to lose my mind?

Zane cursed himself all kinds of stupid when he found himself back at the mental institution the next night, the same one he'd sworn to never visit again. He couldn't even blame it on hunger as he'd fed, quite satisfyingly too, on a pair of muggers.

So why did he find himself perched on the windowsill of the dormitory *she* resided in? The dirty glass made it hard to peer in, as did the bars which while effective for keeping patients in, were no deterrent for someone with his *special* abilities. He hesitated though, not liking the loss of control he exhibited. He cared nothing for mortal matters. He cared naught for human women. Thus, he should not be here.

About to leap back the ground he stopped as he heard the door to the ward click and the soft thud of footsteps. No flashlight preceded the intruder and Zane peered inside, his enhanced eyes taking in the white uniform of the night orderly as he swaggered in the direction of the bed holding the occupant that refused to leave his thoughts. The one who didn't succumb to his brand of magic. The woman he longed to see again.

Unease spread through him as the orderly stopped at her bedside and shone his light in her face.

She's in danger. Not one to question his instincts, Zane applied himself to listening, ready to aid her if need be while pushing aside the question as to why he felt a need to be her champion.

"I'd leave if I were you," she said, sounding not the least bit frightened.

Crazy human. Zane shook his head at her brave words, even as he applauded them.

"I'm the one who gives the orders around here not you," said the night nurse, his tone pompous.

Bet I could make him change his tune. He almost uttered a dark chuckle at the thought.

"Please, you should go before you get hurt." She sounded almost apologetic and Zane wondered at her words. *Does she know I'm here? Is she expecting me to save her?*

"Be nice to me and maybe I'll be nice to you."

"It's not going to happen."

"That's what you think. There's no one here to help you."

She sighed. "Don't say I didn't warn you."

The sound of a zipper was unmistakable and that combined with the conversation dropped a film of red over Zane's gaze. A cold rage descended over him. *She's mine.* He didn't question his sudden ownership, didn't hesitate to act.

Turning his body to mist, he drifted through the bars and screen of the opened window and rematerialized in the room. In mere seconds, he'd grabbed the would-be rapist around the throat and lifted him off the ground.

"Filthy excuse for a human," he growled,

squeezing the meaty neck of the orderly. He cared not if he killed him. Human scum such as this did not deserve to live and walk the earth, not when he was forever confined to stalking the night. How unfair.

Annoyed, he squeezed tighter, letting loose a chuckle as the not-so-tough thug clawed at his hands, his face turning a ruddy shade as he struggled to breath.

To eat or not to eat, that was the question.

Chapter Five

She knew he'd returned a moment before actually seeing him. The voices went silent. Ella held her breath in astonishment as her night visitor of the previous day appeared out of the dark like an avenging angel. With a strength she could barely comprehend—but that excited her—he took care of the orderly before the voices could.

"You came back?" she whispered, the delight evident in her tone while warmth spread through her limbs.

"Good thing I did," he said sounding angry. For her? What a novel concept. "What would you like me to do with this scum?" He shook the man who hung limp in his grasp.

Ella blinked. Do? What could they do? The orderly was sure to tattletale. Even had her voices acted, Ella would still find herself in a bind.

"What can we do? He's going to tell them you came and I'll be put in solitary."

"If they believe him. You could just say he's lying. That you were defending yourself."

She shook her head. "You really have no idea of how things work do you?"

"Apparently not. What would you have preferred? That I let him rape you."

"Oh, the voices would have stopped him. They might have driven me crazy, but they don't let anyone hurt me."

Her shadow savior snorted. "You really are nuts, aren't you?"

Usually hearing it said so baldly didn't bother her, but for some reason hearing it from him caused her to draw in her thin shoulders. "Yes. Yes I am."

"Bloody hell. I knew I should have stayed away." Under his breath, he cursed then with a thump, the body he'd held suspended all this time crumpled to the floor.

"Did you kill him?" She'd be in a lot of trouble if that were the case. No one would believe her if she told them a stranger had entered the ward and done it. Of course, the fact that she lacked the strength to choke a full grown man of his size wouldn't cross their minds. People were funny that way.

"He's not dead, just unconscious." He sounded disgruntled as if he'd preferred the former.

"Oh." Unconscious meant that eventually the night orderly would wake up in a foul mood and if he ran true to previous men of his ilk, he'd take it out on someone. Not her, the voices in her head wouldn't allow it, but some other poor soul who wouldn't understand why they were being punished. The world truly was a cruel place. But she could worry about that later. Right now, she had a guest and as his hostess, it behooved her to make him welcome.

"Can I offer you something? Water? Or a seat..." Her voice trailed off as she peered around only to realize there wasn't even a chair in this new space she called home.

"Are you certain you will be punished

because of this piece of scum?" He nudged the unconscious orderly.

"Probably. But it's not a big deal. It's happened before. It will happen again. It's the way things are and will always be."

"It's not right."

"Right or wrong, doesn't matter. It's who wears the white coats that decide."

"So tell your family. Surely there is someone to advocate for you."

A sad smile tilted her lips. "Not all of us are so lucky to have someone who cares."

Judging by the way his lips thinned and his eyes blazed, he didn't approve of her reply. "So you're just supposed to allow them to abuse you?"

She laughed. "I'm a patient in a mental hospital. What else can I do?"

"Come with me," said her shadowy guest.

Ella sucked in a breath. *Did I just imagine what he said?* She wanted to read his expression, see if he meant it, or if he was merely teasing her, but the gloom kept him faceless. "Excuse me. I think I misunderstood. I thought you said to come with you."

"I did."

"As in leave this place?" A flicker of excitement that she tried to ignore for fear of disappointment, flared to life. "But how? And where will we go?"

"Does it truly matter where so long as we depart this wretched place? You want to leave don't you?"

Leave? Ella stared at his wide cloaked shape in shock, excitement making her tingle. Had the time for the prophecy arrived? She wanted to believe he could get her out, but the sad truth remained, once a person entered the institution, short of a miracle, they never left. Not to mention there were an awful lot of locked doors on the path to freedom. Then again, her mysterious stranger seemed to have no difficulty getting in and out.

"Well?" he asked impatiently.

"But how? The doors are locked and there are orderlies keeping watch. And besides, where will I go once we escape? I have nowhere to hide. No one to take me in." She hated to bring those points up, but Ella knew she'd only get one shot at escape. If she screwed it up and they caught her, they'd lock her up tighter than the crazy guy who tried to light himself on fire.

He sighed. "Trust me. I can get you out and as for the where, I guess you can stay with me until we find you a place of your own. Now, are you ready to meet the real world?"

Was she ever!

Holding out his hand towards her, he waited for her answer. The voices had quieted at his appearance, so she only had herself to rely on-a first. Without even thinking about it, she slipped her hand into his. A simple touch, yet it sent a jolt of awareness through her body and her heart sped up.

Ready or not world, here I come.

Chapter Six

She tucked her hand into his, an electric moment that had him sucking an unneeded breath. What had just happened? Zane didn't know what prompted him to make the offer to help her escape. Chivalry wasn't something he indulged in. Nor did he have time for pity. But still, despite the fact he preferred to show no mercy to anyone, most especially humans, he found himself maneuvering her through the many twists and turns in the dark halls of the mental hospital, because of course, he couldn't just turn her into mist and slip out the window. She was much too solid, temptingly so, for such a feat. But taking the longer route wasn't an issue, his keen senses guided them out and away from those that patrolled the various corridors. Of more pressing concern was his own sanity.

All that patient blood I've ingested over the years really has rendered me nuts. Why else would I be saving a girl who doesn't deny she hears voices? Oh, and let's not forget, she is so crazy she actually thinks the voices would have saved her from rape. Perhaps she's the sane one and I'm the one losing my marbles because why in hell would I tell her she can stay with me?

But even as he thought this, he wouldn't change his decision. He hadn't liked at all the danger that bastard orderly had posed. If he'd left her behind, who would have protected her in the daytime or when he hunted? He didn't understand why he cared about her wellbeing, but he couldn't deny the rage and...possessiveness he felt. *I look at her and all I can think is 'she's mine'.*

How odd and novel. When was the last time a human had stirred him? He couldn't recall, possibly because it had never happened before.

Getting her out of here to explore these unexpected and strange feelings seemed the most logical choice. And if he didn't like the answers, he could always just eat her. But to his shock, instead of seeing himself biting into the smooth, white expanse of her neck, he pictured himself between her white thighs, lapping at her sweet core while she cried out. Zane was thankful the darkness hid his instant and very evident erection.

What a shame, he couldn't dematerialize them both to exit the same way he'd entered, however the trick didn't work on other beings. Using some of the special skills-some would say magical—that he'd acquired over the years, he unlocked the doors that stood in their way. He weaved them a path through the shadows that avoided the humans that kept watch, the rich scent of their blood and life force a beacon he could sense from a distance. But as they approached the side door that the night staff kept unlocked for their smoke breaks, he cursed under his breath. Around the corner from them and steps away from freedom, two burly fellows stood in the way. Eventually they'd discover the girl missing, but he'd prefer it happened once they were far away.

He bent down to whisper to her. "Stay here for a moment." She clung to his hand, the fine bones so fragile in his grasp and yet, despite her obvious frailty, she managed to exude warmth which spread through his undead body. A warmth which did nothing to alleviate his still aroused state. "I need to take care of those two guards."

Biting her lip—something he hoped to do to her later—she let go of his hand and hugged herself. Her pose suggested nervousness, but the brightness in her eyes suggested excitement.

Zane went around the corner and focused on the two humans ahead of him.

"You will go outside and have a cigarette. It's quiet outside. You will see and hear nothing. You will not remember these commands. Go."

As if in a Jedi trance—a phrase that Zane had picked up watching Star Wars—the two staffers eyes glazed over and pivoting, they headed out the door.

"Come," he beckoned her. She peered around the corner then came forward and tucked her hand into his. Her trust in him, made him want to shake her and say *'Don't you realize you should fear me?',* but instead of castigating her, he laced his fingers through hers.

Zane led her through the door to the night outside. The two orderlies smoked without speaking and didn't even turn their heads to look at them. She stared open mouthed at the entranced guards. He could see the question in her eyes, but he shook his head at her before she could voice anything aloud.

When they reached the wall, he turned her to face him. "Place your hands on my shoulders," he ordered as he drew her into his body. His big hands spanned the slimness of her waist easily and the thinness of her gown made him realize how close he was to touching her warm skin. Tucked into his body, she could surely feel the evidence of his desire, yet she didn't remark upon it. Instead, the scent of her arousal wafted up to him like the most decadent of perfumes. *She desires me.* That simple fact shocked him and lust roared through his body. Had he not learned the art of control, he would have taken her then and there like a rutting beast. But he had a bed at home that would provide more comfort, not to mention they hadn't left the grounds of the institution yet.

With a coiling of power, he levitated them, her slight weight not even coming close to taxing the innate magic he'd acquired, just one of many vampiric gifts.

A gasp escaped her as her feet left the ground. Her fingers dug into his shoulders, but she didn't panic. "You can fly! How marvelous." Her obvious enthusiasm made even one as jaded as him smile. She definitely did not react like most humans would.

"I can do *many* things," he whispered in her ear, his loins tightening when she shivered in his arms.

As soon as they hit the ground on the other side of the wall, he let go of her and she stepped back, but he could still hear—and *feel*—her heart racing.

"Now what?" she asked gnawing her lip while peering around her. She appeared wraith like in the dark, seductively so, with the faint illumination of the moon making her skin glow translucently while her hair glimmered a pale silver.

A moon goddess come to life, and his for the taking. A desirable one whose seductive curves were enhanced by the thin gown she wore. He longed to latch his mouth around the pert nipple that poked through the fabric.

Cursing under his breath at his uncontrollable thoughts, Zane pulled out his key fob and hit the unlock button. Lights flashed in the darkness. "Now, we get out of here."

And I introduce you to the mattress in my bedroom.

Chapter Seven

Free. I'm free.

It still stunned her how easily her rescuer accomplished the impossible. Of course, they still needed to remove themselves from the vicinity before someone sounded the alarm, but standing on the side of the road, a road not bound within a gated compound, a road that led to liberty, she couldn't help the elated rush. She spun, her ragged hair spinning around her, laughter bubbling at her lips.

Dizzy and giddy after several revolutions, she stopped and found him regarding her quizzically. "Do you always dance barefoot in the moonlight?"

"No. But I have to say, it's quite nice. This is the first time I've felt moonlight on my skin. I've never been outside at night."

His brows arched. "Never?"

She shook her head. "For the most part, we are kept indoors. It's just easier for the staff that way."

"Unbelievable," he muttered. "We should depart before someone notes your absence. Get in the car." He opened the passenger door and gestured for her to get in.

"With pleasure." The voices returned just as she seated herself in the low slung, leather covered seats. They spoke quickly.

"Stupid girl. What are you doing?"

"Run while you can. Quick before he eats you."

"Freedom at last!" said another while cackling madly with laughter.

She ignored them all except her own voice in her mind which pointed out an interesting fact. "I just realized something. Here you've rescued me, and yet I don't even know your name. I'm Ella."

He tilted his head towards her and she caught the gleam of teeth as he smiled. "Hello, Ella. My name is Zane."

Zane. Ella like the sound of it, but the niceties out of the way, she now had a more important question, one that the voices in unusual tandem shouted at her before shutting up. "Is it true? Are you a vampire?"

The car swerved slightly, and she clutched at the armrests, startled at the motion.

"Why do you say that?" he finally replied tightly.

The voices remained silent, not liking his proximity at all. Ella licked her lips, determined to tell the truth, but knowing, just like all the others, he wouldn't like it. "It's the voices in my head. They told me."

"Really," he said flatly.

"I'm sorry, but I have to ask. Do you drink blood? Is that why you were there the other night? Were you feeding?" The flood of questions poured from her and only when she realized he hadn't responded to any of them did she taper off, uncertainly. *I really just don't know when to shut up,* she thought sadly as she waited for him to freak like everyone in her past had when she spoke truths they thought secret.

"I will answer your questions, Ella of the voices, but in return, you will answer some of mine. Agreed?"

He isn't mad? She smiled in the darkness of his car. "Sure." Ella had nothing to hide. He already knew the world considered her nuts. Anything else he wanted to know would pale in comparison.

"Very well. In answer to your first question, yes, I am a vampire."

Ella bounced in her seat. "Oh, my god. That is so cool. Are you like hundreds of years old? Do—"

*

"Slow down," Zane said with a chuckle and a shake of his head. Her guileless nature and obvious lack of fear intrigued him, but not as much as her obvious arousal at his simple presence. The sweet scent of her teased him, and his lust for her grew. A more impatient man would have pulled over and dragged her into his lap for instant gratification, but Zane liked to think he had better control than that. Of course, being in command of his libido didn't mean he didn't push the speed limit for this road, weaving the mostly unlit route with a skill usually seen on a racetrack. She didn't seem to mind. Her excitement at his vampiric nature making her oblivious to the fact they raced at twice the recommended speed.

Her questions continued to fire at him unabated. "Do you turn into a bat? Does your heart beat?" She paused to take a breath.

In the gap, he took his chance to interrupt

34

her. "Slow down. I will answer your questions one at a time if you but give me a chance." He didn't mind assuaging her curiosity, not now when he had her in his possession. The only way she'd leave him now would be in death. But he hoped to not have to resort to that until he'd enjoyed many a taste.

"Sorry." She ducked her head. "I got a little excited."

He chuckled. "A little?"

"Okay, a lot. But in my defense, you're the most exciting thing that's ever happened to me."

Whose ego wouldn't inflate at those words? Only to deflate as he reminded himself it came from a woman certifiably crazy who'd lived incarcerated. "Let's start with the basics. As a vampire, I drink blood to survive. Human blood that is. Animal blood can be substituted in extreme cases," such as when he found himself hunted and needed to lay low and hidden. But that was in his early days, before he learned to better hide who he was. "I try not to kill my victims in order to not draw attention to myself. I keep a handful of blood donors at the house to satisfy my needs."

"And yet you were at the hospital eating. Why?"

"Like a human, sometimes I like to dine out. I use places like mental hospitals and long term facility care places for patients in comas and whatnot to feed myself when I'm in the mood for variety. I spread my feeding among multiple humans, most of whom can't talk or if they can, are considered crazy if they do. Little tastes here and there that leave no lasting effect or sign."

"Ooh, so would you have bitten me then

had I not talked to you the other night?" She sounded breathless and the scent of her arousal increased, filling the car.

So sweet..."That was the intention yes. Now, your turn. How long have you been institutionalized?"

"Forever."

Her answer took him aback. "You jest?"

"Okay, not forever. Since I was seven years old."

"Who puts a child in an asylum?" He blurted the query aloud, unable to help himself.

"My parents did."

The answer appalled him. "But why? What grievous act did you perform to make them do such a drastic thing?" For surely she'd done something utterly reprehensible to merit such a punishment. The idea that beneath her veneer of innocence lurked something dark intrigued rather than repelled him.

"The voices made me ask my dad why he was cheating on my mom. Needless to say, that didn't go over well. My parents split up and neither wanted me, so they had me put away. I've been there ever since."

What no murder? No blood? She'd simply called her father out on his infidelity? A righteous indignation he'd not felt in a long time stirred in him. Zane, who'd seen quite a bit in his lifetime—lots of it not pretty—could barely credit the callous disregard her parents had shown her. "How old are you now?"

"Twenty five."

So young in comparison to him. "You say

these voices you hear, they told these things? Just like they told you what I am?"

She nodded.

"And have you always heard these voices?"

"As far back as I can remember. Sometimes they do things too."

"Like?" She'd implied previously that the voices she heard could act, but surely that claim was a part of her madness.

Blonde locks went flying as she shook her head. "Enough about me. Your turn again. How old are you?"

Zane grinned at her, a flash of fang that didn't cause her to recoil. "Very old."

She cocked her head and peered at him, her eyes going slightly out of focus. "Three hundred and twenty seven."

Once again, the car swerved and Zane shot Ella an incredulous look. *How did she guess?* "Why that number?"

"It's what the voices say."

"I thought you said they went away when I was around."

"They have, but when I asked them just now, one of them answered."

A niggling thought made him say, "Are you sure you're crazy?"

Ella giggled. "What would make you think I wasn't? Only crazy people hear voices."

"Okay, let me ask you a different question. Are the voices always right?"

She didn't immediately answer and he looked over at her and saw her staring at her hands clasped in her lap. It took her several moments before she replied softly. "They're never wrong. It's why I get into so much trouble."

The sadness he heard made him want to hurt someone, make that a lot of someones. Although, why he even cared eluded him. He barely knew the chit. What did he care how others treated her? But he did care. Cared more than he understood, and on top of that, the curiosity within him, before a mere flicker, flared into full flamed life as an idea formed in his mind, *What if she's not crazy?* Could there be something to her madness, forces at play that no one suspected. Possible. He'd have to take her to a friend to test that theory. Later though. First things first. Given the state of his cock— turgid—and his hunger-voracious—he needed to take care of himself first.

Answering a few more questions for her— no, he did not turn into a bat; no, crosses didn't burn; and yes, he owned a coffin, he just didn't sleep in it—made the voyage to his home pass quickly. As he slowed to a crawl before a gated wall, the wrought iron entrance swung open, recognizing the signal his vehicle emitted. He cleared the gate and purred up the long drive to a sprawling mansion. He parked in front of the tiered steps and quicker than a human could blink, had exited the car and opened the door on her side. He held out his hand in invitation.

Ella tendered him a shy smile and slid her fingers without hesitation into his, the tingle of flesh to flesh instant. Anticipation made his blood quicken and his loins tighten. It wouldn't be long now. In the master suite on the second level, his bed awaited. How he longed to see her stripped and laid bare upon the black satin, her creamy skin a perfect compliment. His mouth practically watered and his canines pushed painfully, his vampiric nature unable to completely control its excitement at tasting her blood.

Only moments away from the seduction, he fought an inner battle to not sweep her into his arms and race to his room. *Think of it as foreplay.* His cock seemed more of a mind that it was torture.

His unseemly hunger for her bothered him. He couldn't recall ever feeling so out of control before. So needy of a human. It seemed to take her forever to step from his car and even longer to get her up the steps as she paused to gape around her at the splendor he took for granted. He schooled himself to not show his impatience. Soon, he'd have her naked in his arms and hopefully this obsession he had for her would dissipate. *I hope.*

Chapter Eight

Subtle outdoor lighting highlighted the exterior of Zane's impressive home. No doubt about it, the vampire wasn't hurting financially. She'd watched her share of movies and shows over the years, severely censored of course to avoid inciting the other patients, so she knew what she looked at wasn't the norm for most people. But then again, Zane wasn't a normal person. *He's a vampire.*

The idea titillated her. She'd read Bram Stoker's 'Dracula', a gift from a nurse who'd smuggled it in to her, one of the few people she'd encountered who'd treated her like she was just a regular person. Sadly, they'd transferred Nurse Kelly and the books had stopped, but Ella had never forgotten the dark tale of the being who survived on blood—*and who loved.*

Ella knew it was the height of foolishness to think Zane had saved her because of some instant love for her. Her life wasn't a fairy tale, and Zane wasn't a prince come to rescue his princess. But, that didn't stop Ella from fantasizing a little. Surely she was allowed. Surely she'd earned the right. In all of her life, nothing this exciting had ever happened to her. Even the occasional chocolate pudding paled in comparison to just one chuckle or smile from her dark rescuer. The small pleasures she'd treasured before, hot showers, candy, the occasional book, paled when it came to the thrill of his touch. A touch she couldn't help wanting. *And I want it on more than just my hand.* Of that, her body, heart and mind agreed. If she were to only have one chance at sex, then she wanted it to be with him, a man who made her whole body tingle and sing, every moment with him a sensory pleasure like she'd never imagined.

From the car she stepped, toward a future unknown. The voices screamed she was being foolish. They shut up as Zane took her hand and tugged her up the steps to the grand wooden doors leading into the magnificent house. As if by magic, the portals swung open and at Zane's urging, she stepped inside. Turned out it wasn't magic but a real butler who'd opened the door, almost as fantastical.

Shyness overcame her, and she stepped closer to Zane, his electric presence easing her as the elderly gent who'd let them in looked her over with dispassionate eyes. Over the years she'd become used to people looking right through her.

"Hendricks, this is Ella. She will be staying here for a while. Please advise the staff that I want her treated with the utmost courtesy. Also, she'll require meals, so ensure the kitchen is stocked and that all are made aware of my orders." Zane gave orders to his servant, orders to treat her well and she could have kissed him for his attention and care. A part of her warned she should be more leery of his kindness—*he wants something of you.* Blood more than likely, and he was welcome to it. While a part of her understood Zane's vampiric state should frighten her, she couldn't help but trust him. *He is the savior from my dream. How can I not trust him?* Besides, the warmth that suffused her whenever she found herself in his presence felt too good to be wrong.

"I will notify the staff and have chef meet with her in the morning to prepare a meal plan."

"Oh, there's no need for that. I don't want to be a bother."

"It's not a bother, ma'am. Please feel free to call upon me if you require anything." The butler bowed, to her eternal embarrassment.

Unused to nice treatment, Ella's cheeks bloomed with color. Zane chuckled. "I think our guest is a little overwhelmed."

A little? Try a lot.

"Will that be all, Master?" asked the sober butler.

"Yes, you may retire."

The butler pivoted around and began to walk away when Zane cursed. "Hendricks," he called.

"Master?" said the servant who stopped before going through the door he'd opened.

"Clothes. Ella will need clothing. I trust you can ensure she is outfitted properly?"

"As you wish." With a bow and another speculative glance her way, Hendricks left them alone.

Ella found herself tongue tied, baffled at Zane's actions and afraid she'd say something to ruin this dream—and even more afraid the voices would do something to ruin it. She'd not kidded when she said they liked to act. But they remained silent for the moment. She was on her own. With a vampire. A vampire she'd never clearly seen given they'd traveled for the most part in darkness.

Curious about her benefactor, she peeked up at him and for the first time got the full impact of his face.

Oh my god, he's gorgeous. At last, she had a face for her dream savior—and fantasy lover.

Piercing black eyes framed by decadently long lashes held hers. His face defined the term chiseled with a strong, square jaw, a straight aristocratic nose and a surprising olive complexion, if a pale one. She found herself transfixed, from his slightly ruffled black hair, to his full lips that quirked in a smile.

"Enjoying the view?" He raised a brow at her and grinned even wider when she blushed hotly. She caught a glimpse of white teeth, and more interestingly, two pointed canines.

But back to her initial thought before he'd distracted her with his good looks. "You don't have to do all this."

Zane frowned at her. "I know I don't. I choose to. You are my guest. It is my duty as host to ensure you are properly taken care of. Now come. Let me show you my home." With obvious pride of possession, and while holding her hand which just made the warmth invading her limbs grow hotter, Zane gave her a tour of the house from the magnificent and cavernous living room, to the mystifying and gleaming kitchen. A conservatory, library, massive dining room and even larger reception room took up the first floor. On the second floor, there was an entertainment room with a television so big she wondered how they'd gotten it in the room. A multitude of guest bedrooms lay behind a hallway of doors, each sumptuous and larger than she'd ever imagined someone needing.

Finally, he showed her a bedroom draped in reds and blacks, its bed massive and a huge window with heavy drapes pulled back to let in the moonlight. His room, she surmised as she spotted the silken robe lying across the bed.

Pulling free of his hand, she wandered to the middle of the room and ran a finger down the satiny comforter on the bed. The voices came back in a rush.

"Oh dear girl, you've entered his lair."
"Stake him."
"Run before he debauches you!"
"Ooh, someone's about to get lucky…"

Ella's brow crinkled at the conflicting commands. The voices quieted abruptly when Zane grabbed her by the arms.

"Are you okay?"

"I am now. My little friends upstairs don't like you and they were just letting me know."

"They stop talking when I touch you?" he asked, the grip on her arms loosening and sliding so that he held her in a loose hug.

It didn't even occur to Ella to push him away. The soothing relief his touch brought from the voices not to mention the heat that infused her body made her lean into him. "Actually, so long as I'm fairly near to you they shut up."

"Then we'll have to ensure you stay close to my side," he murmured in a low voice. "Very close." His hands dropped to her bottom, and drew her closer, pressing her against his lower body.

Her eyes widened as she felt the hardness of him, unmistakable and flattering. *He desires me!* Up until now she'd wondered. Hoped.

Tilting her head back, she glanced at him to see if she could read his mood and make sure she wasn't mistaken. Hooded eyes peered down at her. Zane raised his hand and with one finger, stroked her lips, tracing them, teasing them. Light headed and mesmerized by his touch, Ella's lips parted. As if this were a signal he'd waited for, his head dipped down. Closing her eyes, she waited for her first kiss.

And oh, the fire it ignited.

Gently he brushed her mouth, sliding his lips across hers, a cautious exploration. Ella, inexperienced but curious, and desiring for the first time in her life, tentatively pressed back. His arms tightened around her and he deepened the kiss, his lips tugging and tasting hers. The flick of his tongue made her gasp and he used that to his advantage, slipping his tongue into her mouth to twine with hers. Ella's knees buckled, but he held her up, crushing her against his hard body, igniting a fire between her legs.

Ella vaguely understood what was happening. She'd seen patients coupling with each other in the wards. Heard and seen the orderlies indulge, she'd just never participated herself. She'd never wanted to. Never, until Zane.

A sharp canine nicked her lower lip and the metallic tang of her blood hit her tongue, a flavor that seemed to enflame Zane because he moved them backwards in the direction of the bed even as his hands tugged at her flimsy gown, sliding it up over her hips to bare her buttocks.

Eager even in her uncertainty, Ella knew she needed to tell him before things went any further. She just hoped it wouldn't make a difference.

"Zane," she panted pulling away from his eager mouth.

"No more questions, Ella. I want you and I know you want me to. I can sense your arousal."

His words made her tremble. *Wanted.* She could feel the proof against her lower belly and her reciprocal desire in the wetness that made her panties wet. But, he needed to know. She hoped he'd consider what she had to say a gift. "I want you too. I just wanted to say, I'm glad you're going to be my first."

Chapter Nine

Not much shocked Zane. When you'd lived as long as him, there was little left that surprised. But, with just a few words, Ella managed. Zane froze a hairsbreadth from her lips, even though his body screamed at him to claim her—and not just with his cock. Perhaps he'd misunderstood. "I'm sorry. Are you saying what I think you are? You're a virgin?"

Eyes bright, she nodded at him and smiled. "The voices never let men get near me, not that I ever wanted to before you. And I know we just met and all, but you make me feel ever so wonderful. From what I've learned over the years, I know it's going to hurt a little and I'm fine with that. I just thought I should warn you."

Holy shit. Zane withdrew his hands from her and backed away in shock. He couldn't decide if he liked this unexpected development or cursed it. *Untouched. Pure.* The savage in him exulted and clamored to claim her, to put his undeniable mark on her flesh. But to his surprise, a shred of humanity that he'd thought lost forever rose up and admonished him to leave her be. How dare he sully her? After what she'd been through, she deserved better. A chance to live, to gift her innocence to someone who would cherish it, and her.

Of all the times for his forgotten morals to rear their bloody head…

Slowly, he retreated from her, trying to ignore the taste of her essence on his tongue, a lingering ambrosia from when he'd nicked her. He willed himself to forget the softness and yielding of her body in his arms. He tried to pretend the air wasn't perfumed with the sweet smell of her arousal. He tried to resist temptation.

"You should leave."

The longing in her clear blue eyes turned to uncertainty and questions clouded them. "You don't want me?"

If only that were the case. A fluttering touch at his back had him tensing. He whirled and grabbed her hands lest her innocent gesture send him over the edge. "No," he said firmly.

"I don't understand. Is it because I'm a virgin? I would have thought you'd be pleased." She appeared confused and he longed to kiss her and show her how much her words enflamed him.

"Why would you want to gift me with that? You do realize I am a creature of the night. I am not human like you are. I could drain you of your blood and not feel a moment's remorse."

"Oh, I get you're not human, but I don't think you'd kill me." She tugged her hands free and pressed her palms against his chest. Eyes shining with trust looked up at him. His usually still heart hitched. "You saved me. That's not the act of a killer."

"I saved you for my own selfish reasons."

"Because you want me."

"You know nothing."

"I might not be experienced, but I know that you desire me. I felt it."

"A hard cock means nothing. I am a vampire. The blood lust often translates into arousal."

"Then I don't see the problem. You get what you want, and I get what I want."

"You just escaped. You don't know what you want."

Her lips pursed and her eyes flashed. An invisible breeze ruffled the ragged ends of her hair. "Don't think to tell me what I want. For years, I've lived like a prisoner. Never knowing desire. Never understanding it. You come along and now suddenly I have all these feelings inside me. Urges."

"It is only because you are grateful."

She laughed, a tinkling sound he enjoyed too much. "Grateful yes, but I've been grateful to other people over the years, it doesn't mean I wanted to share myself with them. I want this, Zane. I want you. Please. I know you've already done so much for me, freeing me and all. Please grant me one more gift. Give me passion."

He couldn't help but groan at her plea, the burning touch of her hands through the fabric of his shirt making him forget his reasons for abstaining. "The devil knows I want you. Your very innocence is what makes you so tempting, but at the same time, it is very possible that I will lose control." In the throes of passion, the breaking of her maidenhead and the purity of the blood released... it would be beyond pleasurable, and dangerous. And here she almost begged him to do it.

Again, she flashed the smile which he already found himself addicted to. "I think you exaggerate."

"And if I don't? I could accidentally kill you."

"So you will bite me?" she asked as she slid her hands up to his shoulders and again, stepped closer to him.

"Most definitely," he whispered, mesmerized by her, his lust close to overwhelming his reason.

"Does it hurt?" she asked licking her lips, the sweet musky scent of her arousal floating in a cloud around them and making it hard for him to remember why this was a bad idea.

"Only for a second, then you'll experience unbelievable bliss."

"Sounds like a winning situation for both of us." Tilting her head back, she exposed the long, unmarked column of her neck. Zane trembled, his usual cynicism and mastery of all situations blown away by her simple trusting act.

Leaning forward, he let his lips graze the skin she offered, the pulsing of an artery causing him to salivate. To hunger. He could resist no longer. Lips clamped to her offered skin, he sucked at the tender flesh, not yet breaking it, savoring the moment. She moaned. Wrapping her in his arms, he lifted her and moved her towards the bed. If he was going to do this, then he would do it right. He wanted to be inside her when he bit her, her sweet life's blood pouring on his tongue as he plunged his cock inside her sex. Oh, the ecstasy of it. The thrill. The...

Something hit him on the back of the head, a hard blow. With a curse, he let her go and whirled.

"Who's there?" he snapped. "Show

yourself," he demanded as he scrutinized every corner, seeking the intruder who dared invade his private quarters—and interrupt his seduction.

No one appeared nor did he sense anyone, but that didn't stop the loose bric-a-brac in his room from lifting on its own and sailing at him, missiles launched by invisible hands.

What the hell is going on?

Chapter Ten

Talk about miserable luck. Ella could only watch in frustration as the voices in her head took action, ruining a moment she'd dreamt of for years. "Stop it!" she cried. "Stop your antics right this minute!" Hands planted on her hips, she chastised her friends in the attic while Zane tossed her the oddest look.

The voices however were in no mood to listen. As a matter of fact, and perhaps because of their extended silence, they had quite a bit to say, and they screamed it in her head.

"Run while he's distracted."

"Wicked slut!"

"We'll save you from his debauchery."

But I want this, she thought with a growl at her constant companions.

"No!" they all wailed, a crowd of personalities united in the moment.

My body, my choice, she mentally snapped back. Apparently, that didn't count. Things continued to rise and launch themselves at Zane.

"The voices are doing this?" asked Zane as he blocked the lamp that flew at him. It crashed to the floor and glass sprayed all over.

She nodded her head and sighed. *Great, now he's probably going to tell me to leave. I finally find someone who interests me and doesn't treat me like a freak and my little friends had to ruin it. Happy now?* she snarled at them.

Masculine laughter filled the room, a rich and compelling sound. Startled, Ella looked around for the source only to realize it was Zane chuckling, even as he dodged more missiles.

"What's so funny?" she asked, crinkling her face in confusion.

"This," he said, whirling to bat down the books that sailed at him with flapping pages. "I mean in my youth, we had iron chastity belts to keep maidens pure, but this is new. And entertaining." He smiled at her with sharp teeth, not at all bothered by her voices poltergeist act.

Oh my god, he's crazy. Just like me. Ella couldn't help but beam in relief that he was taking the unplanned attack so well.

The voices didn't like his attitude and alternated between sulking and wailing. Rising from the bed, she walked over to him. He opened his arms wide, offering her a safe haven, letting the last few missiles hit him without even a single pained grunt.

With an exasperated, collective sigh, the voices shut up and the remaining floating objects dropped to the floor. Ella rubbed her cheek against the soft linen of his shirt, his male scent, part cologne, part him, making her want to purr—among other things.

"So what now?" she asked. Given the violent outburst of her voices, was she doomed to a life of virginity? *I hope not.* Especially since the small sampler she'd gotten of passion made her long for more.

"I think we'd better wait to indulge in our

passions until we find a solution to your poltergeist problem. I'd hate for all the maids to quit at the mess they have to clean up. Not to mention, I have quite a few priceless antiques that I would prefer to keep intact."

"I'm sorry."

"For what?"

"What do you think? For causing so much trouble. For making such a mess. For thinking I could finally have a life." Ella made a moue that he couldn't see but apparently sensed.

"Who said I was giving up?"

"You saw what happened. I'm doomed to be a lonely virgin the rest of my life."

He laughed. "The horror."

"This isn't funny."

"I'm sure you don't think so at the moment, but eventually you will look back upon this moment and laugh."

"Says the man who doesn't have to live with it," she grumbled.

"And what if you didn't have to either?"

"What do you mean?" Brow knit in a frown of confusion, she peeked up at him.

"I have a theory about your little friends, and if I'm right, you will be mine very soon."

Ella's body flushed with pleasure at his words and he groaned, tightening his arms around her.

"Aaah Ella, you make me want to tempt a concussion." His lips brushed the top of her head, and she snuggled tighter against him. "But, just in case they resort to sharper objects, we should abstain. At the very least until I can prepare a room without any danger to either of us."

"You mean like a padded cell?"

He laughed. "That's not a bad idea actually. But, hopefully we can do better than that. Just not tonight. The night is coming to a close. I shall show you to a room that you might rest."

"Can't I stay with you?" she begged. "Please. I don't want to listen to the voices."

He hesitated. "Very well. But I warn you, once the dawn lightens the sky, I will become as a corpse, my heart almost stopping and my skin becoming chill. You may find this frightening."

"I don't care. Please Zane, let me sleep with you."

This time he didn't answer, just swept her up and carried her to the bed. Pulling back the covers, she slid onto satin sheets and waited for him to join her, ignoring the voices that gibbered in her head. With a tilt of his lips Zane stripped, his linen shirt getting tossed on to a chair and showing off a muscular torso with almost no hair. To think, she'd come so close to being able to touch that ivory skin. Ella couldn't stop a blush when his hands tugged at the button of his pants. Modesty prevailed and she turned her head, but she still heard his chuckle and the rustle of fabric as he removed his slacks.

The light in the room went out and he slid into bed beside her. His hands, cooler than earlier, reached out to touch her, and he didn't have to tug her much for her to snuggle herself against him, the voices silencing at his touch. She rested a hand on his chest, the soft, slow thud of his heart relaxing her.

For the first time in a long time, she

understood what it felt like to belong somewhere, to feel wanted. Not alone. To have her mind empty of voices and thoughts, or at least those not belonging to her. It was peaceful.

Was that the only reason she wanted Zane though? Because he could stem the madness in her mind? As she lay there, cocooned in his arms, she thought about it. While the tranquility was nice, there was more to her attraction to Zane than just his ability to mute the voices. He attracted her. He intrigued her. Her heart skipped a beat when he spoke or smiled at her. Her skin tingled when he was near. Her tummy fluttered when he touched her.

Vampire or not, I want him. I will find a way to have him and stop the voices from interfering. I won't let them ruin this for me. I've finally got a chance to live, and I won't give it up, not without a fight.

Chapter Eleven

Am I suicidal?

Over three hundred years old, usually paranoid about his safety, and yet here he was agreeing to let Ella sleep with him. What insanity did he suffer from? Had she cast a spell upon him? He could see no logical explanation to explain why he trusted a mental patient who heard voices and had poltergeist activity protecting her virtue.

Of all the things he'd seen over the years, that incident ranked high on his weird-o-meter. Fathers with shotguns, boyfriends with fists, crying maidens, and yes, even archaic chastity belts, he'd seen and heard of them all, but flung items, by invisible hands? How unique, just like Ella.

Unused to sharing his quarters so close to dawn, Zane lay alongside her and listened as her breathing evened out signaling her descent into deep slumber. Her hand lay over his heart while her head nestled in the hollow of his shoulder. So intimate and peaceful. Dare he even say welcome?

A multitude of emotions battled in him, from exhilaration at her closeness, to trepidation at the trust he put in this woman he barely knew. He also found himself wanting to be more than just a vampire, a devourer of blood and souls. For the first time since he'd turned, he'd come across someone who looked upon him as more than a monster or someone to be feared. When Ella gazed upon him, she saw a man and protector. She placed her faith in him. Wanted him. Holding her close as the sun rose over the horizon, his limbs grew heavy, his thoughts clouded as his life left his body, but he couldn't help but smile as he slipped into a daring dream. A fantasy really, for a life where the loneliness he'd suffered since his turning no longer existed. Where he could have someone at his side to share the pleasures life—or un-life—had to offer. A future with Ella.

He just hoped he hadn't misjudged her. It would suck to wake up with a stake in his heart.

Chapter Twelve

The insistent beeping of his cellphone signaling a text message woke Dr. Peters. Rubbing his face, he groped for the electronic device on his nightstand. He read the text marked urgent and cursed.

Within the hour, he was at the asylum and had the night orderly in his office.

"Tell me again what happened," the doctor demanded in his sternest voice.

The man, named Jimmy, fidgeted in the chair. "I was just doing my rounds, you know. Same as usual when, someone jumped me from behind and choked me 'til I passed out." Jimmy rubbed at the purple bruises on his throat, marks that spoke a slightly different tale. Whoever left them did so from the front, not the back. And, given their span, were too big to have been caused by one slip of a girl, a girl that was now missing.

"And that's all you remember?"

"Yeah."

"According to the security guard doing the rounds, you were found lying by a patient's bed, inside a dorm room, a patient, I might add, who cannot be located."

Jimmy's eyes slid away from Dr. Peters. "I, um, heard something and was checking it out. That's when the guy jumped me."

Dr. Peters slammed his hand down on the

desk. The loud crack made Jimmy jump. "Liar! Did you really think I didn't know about your night time activities? I've turned a blind eye to them, but you were specifically warned to stay away from the girl and you disobeyed me."

"I wasn't. I swear. I didn't touch. You gotta bel--." The doctor muttered something under his breath and squeezed his fist. Jimmy's eyes bulged as he clutched at his throat, gasping for air.

Leaning back in his seat, Dr. Peters smiled as he watched the male nurse writhe. "Because you couldn't keep it in your pants the girl is missing. We don't know if she left on her own or if someone took her. When it comes to your story about a stranger on the ward, your story might hold a grain of truth. But I can't know for sure, as it seems someone turned off the cameras so he could indulge himself, leaving us without any clues." It also left him with a huge mess to deal with. Missing patients were bad news. "I've had enough of your incompetence. I don't like liars and I especially don't like people who fail me. Enjoy yourself in hell." Tighter, he wound his fist, until his nails dug crescents in the palm of his hand.

Jimmy's eyes rolled up in his head and he fell off the chair onto the floor with a loud thump, his head tilting at an odd angle.

Dr. Peters got up and stepped around the warm corpse. He left his office and signaled the man who waited outside.

"Sir?"

"Take care of the body. Discreetly of course. Then gather some men. I want the girl found. She can't have gone far." If she left alone. If she had help though… But who? Who would help her? She'd not had contact with anyone other than staff for years according to her patient file. Even her parents didn't communicate with her. *Maybe I'm not the only one interested in her voices.*

Dr. Peters left rather than supervise the clean-up of the body. No one would dare disobey him or they'd face the consequences. Something Jimmy learned the hard way.

He strode through the halls to the ward Ella had disappeared from. The patients with whom she'd shared the room had been moved for the night so that he could do some investigative work of his own.

With the cameras not recording, he couldn't verify the orderly's account. Not that it mattered. He'd warned the pervert to stay away from Ella. All of them were to leave her alone. One simple command, and yet the incompetents working for him still fucked it up, and the prize he'd searched for all these years was gone.

Missing.

For the moment.

Thankfully, there were other ways of piecing together what happened, and hopefully locating her.

Standing with his legs slightly spread, Dr. Peters lifted his arms and closed his eyes. He drew on the power he'd stolen from another, one like Ella. The gibbering of voices screamed as he pulled on the force that animated them. A cool wind blew through the room and when he opened his eyes, he watched the bleary movie of Ella's departure. His eyes widened slightly in surprise at the cloaked being that had choked his man.

What do you know, he spoke the truth.

His lips tightened in anger when he saw how eagerly Ella departed with the indistinct stranger.

The image faded and Dr. Peters, more commonly known as Marcus in the magic circles he frequented, cast another spell.

A smoky form coalesced in front of him, writhing as if in agony. Like he cared.

"I hurt. I hurt so much. Set me free," the ghost pleaded.

"You're dead. The dead feel nothing."

"Wrong. So wrong. Wrong about so many things." The spirit twisted and pulled at the command which tethered him, but Marcus held tight, even as the sweat beaded on his brow.

"I want the name of the man who took her."

The ghost grimaced. "Man, there was no man."

Marcus frowned. His stolen magic was siphoning out of him quickly, he needed an answer now. Twisting the binding, the spirit he'd summoned screamed. "Answer me with the truth," Marcus ordered.

"I speak truly," whimpered the soul that had once been a man, but now found itself caught in limbo and at the mercy of those like Marcus who could harness their energy for his own use. "The creature you see is not a man, but a soul stealer."

Marcus frowned. "Explain."

"You would know them as vampire."

Marcus in his surprise lost his hold over the ghost which immediately dissipated into the ether he'd pulled it from.

A vampire. A prize as great as Ella. But now,

how to find him? Perhaps one of his magical grimoires at home, many dating back thousands of years, would have more information for him. A tracking spell would be nice.

Excitement made him smile, not a pretty sight, but one which Ella thankfully didn't see else she might not have slept so soundly.

Chapter Thirteen

Ella woke to dead silence. Literally. Her constant mind companions absent, the body she lay against cool to the touch, and the heart beat that had put her to sleep, absent. Had she been made of weaker stuff, she might have cried out, but Ella had spent most of her life in a place where death seemed more normal than some of the things she'd seen and experienced. Easing out from Zane's loosely draped arms, she wiggled to a seated position in the bed.

The room would have been pitch black had it not been for a small bedside lamp that hadn't been there when she went to sleep. Its soft light lit the features of her unlikely rescuer.

In repose—or should she say death—his features had softened. The harsh, cynical lines she'd noted smoothed away and displaying his actual youthfulness. Well at least in looks. He'd implied he was quite old, something the voices had confirmed, and she assumed that his diet of blood was part of what kept him looking young.

What she still hadn't figured out was why the voices disappeared when she touched or got close to him. And yet they'd come back, in action at least, when they thought he would be seducing and biting her. Was there something about Zane that blocked them or judging by their erratic rants, did he frighten them?

Is my mind manifesting the fear I should feel? No,

that makes no sense because I honestly don't think I have anything to fear from him. A connection, make that an awareness, existed between them. Their fascination with each other seemed mutual, and having lived a sheltered life for so long Ella didn't intend to question or stop it.

I am finally getting the chance to live—perhaps find love? Love, an emotion she'd longed for all her life. She wondered what it would feel like. *Is Zane, a vampire, capable of that emotion?* Or an even better question, would he allow himself to?

Her bladder made its presence known and much as she wanted to stay cuddled by his side, she knew she had to take care of it before she embarrassed herself.

The voices invaded her mind as soon as she moved away from the bed.

"Now's your chance. Leave while he sleeps."

"Stake the evil one."

"'Ware the doctor."

The doctor comment caught her attention. *What doctor?* she asked, but the voices just babbled and she ignored them. She opened several doors in his room before finding the bathroom.

His ensuite gleamed, a thing of marble and mirrors with a huge tub. After relieving herself, she looked in the mirror and cringed. Her hair, a washed out blonde color, circled her head in a snarly mess. Eying the tub, she decided a bath was called for. His bedside clock had shown the time to be early afternoon. If he held true to most legends, he wouldn't rise for a few hours still.

Stripping out of the hated hospital gown, she stuffed it in a garbage can. She'd wear nothing before she'd put that thing back on.

The hot water she sank into closely resembled heaven and she closed her eyes, humming happily to herself as she soaped herself, the babble of voices unable to ruin this moment of blissful serenity. She only vaguely remembered baths from her youth. At the hospital, it had always been quick showers, closely supervised by staff. Her lack of prudishness was probably what saved her from screaming when the bathroom door open, and an expressionless Hendricks entered with a pile of clothing which he lay on the bathroom counter.

Looking at a point well above her head, he announced. "When milady has finished her bath, breakfast awaits her downstairs."

Ella bit her lip to hold in her giggles at his stiff posture as he pivoted and left. She soaked in the bath a few more minutes before yanking the plug and getting out. She wrapped herself in a decadently plush towel that smelled like flowers. Rubbing herself dry, she took a peek at the clothes Hendricks brought her.

There were a pair of lace red panties that made her blush, but which she pulled on. A pair of slim fitting track pants with a matching zip up sweater. A white t-shirt completed the rest of her outfit, their stiffness attesting to their newness. The clothes fit a bit loosely, but having only ever worn the very used and ugly garb of the institution, she smiled in delight. Padding back out to the bedroom in socked feet-yes, Hendricks had even remembered those—she gnawed her lip indecisively. The room still lay in a thick gloom and Zane slept like the dead. Ella stifled a giggle, but couldn't stop the growl of hunger which just about echoed in the still room.

Trepidation in her step, she crossed to the door that led to the rest of the house. The voices seemed to approve of this plan because they still exhorted her to escape. Ella didn't plan to leave, but she did need to eat. Taking a deep breath for courage, she left Zane's room in search of the breakfast Hendricks said waited for her.

She noticed the hallway bore no windows, but evenly spaced lighting chased away the darkness. She followed the corridor back to the stairs. The main floor didn't seem to have the same ban on natural light as the upstairs did, because she walked down the gleaming wooden steps into sunlight. She blinked at the brightness. Peering through the windows, she could just see the sun setting, the sky a rainbow of colors.

As if he'd just materialized out of nowhere, Hendricks appeared at her elbow and she almost screamed. Someone really should tie a bell on the man.

"If milady would follow me." The butler led the way to the giant dining room she'd seen in her previous night's tour.

One lonely plate with a silver dome sat on the immense wooden table's surface. Hendricks held out the chair and looked at her, but Ella hesitated.

"I don't suppose there is somewhere a little less fancy to eat is there?"

Hendricks arched an imperious brow, and Ella blushed. "I'm sorry. I guess I should thank you first for the clothes. I've never owned anything so fine before. And as for eating, I don't want to be any trouble."

Before Ella could seat herself at a table meant for royalty, Hendricks face softened. "I was about to have bite myself in the kitchen. Would you prefer to join me there?"

"Oh, please." Ella's face brightened and before Hendricks could change his mind, she snagged the domed plate, while Hendricks grabbed the utensils and glass of juice.

She followed him back to the kitchen where she perched herself at the counter. Hendricks wasn't the only one to join her, a plump matron with rosy cheeks and a smile also bustled over.

"So you're the lamb the master's brought home. My name is Anna. I am the cook and housekeeper."

"My name is Ella, ma'am."

"Ma'am. Goodness child, call me Anna. Do you mind if I ask how you came to know the master?"

Zane hadn't told her to keep quiet and the voices seemed to like his two servants because they shouted no warnings, on the contrary, one of them hummed a happy song. "Zane saved me and said I could stay here until I was settled."

"Saved you from what, lamb?"

"The mental hospital."

Hendricks went into a choking fit beside her and Anna quickly rounded the counter to pound on his back. Wheezing, he looked at her with piercing eyes. "Are you crazy then?"

"Apparently," said Ella with a shrug. "I hear voices."

Anna's eyes lit up. "How fascinating."

"Not really," grumbled Ella. "They tend to be noisy and get me into trouble."

Anna chuckled. "But I'll bet life is never dull though. Now that you are free, what do you intend to do?"

"She's going to accompany me on an outing to test a theory."

"Zane!" Ella jumped off her stool and ran to him enthusiastically, his arms opening just in time for her hurtling body. She hugged him tight. "I'm so happy to see you."

Hendricks choked again.

Chapter Fourteen

"A good evening to you too." Zane dropped a kiss on her forehead and Ella beamed as if given the best present. Even better, none of the kitchen knives took a stab.

Flabbergasted looks marked his employee's faces. Anna and Hendricks had been with him a long time. He could see the curiosity, the amazement and yes the mirth they fought to control. This was the first time anyone, especially a human, had ever shown such obvious enthusiasm for his presence. *And I like it.*

When he'd woken and noticed Ella missing, he'd almost left the room in a naked rush to find her. Only the thought of what his people would say if they saw him rushing about like a crazed man had made him stop long enough to dress. Given the sun hadn't fully set, he'd had to resort to the back staircase and halls to avoid the still setting sun streaming through the front windows.

Luckily, she proved easy to find, and just as adorable as he recalled. He couldn't help but hug her back. He scowled at the grin on Anna's face, a scowl that widened when she mouthed, "About time."

A busy bodying mother hen, sometimes he wondered why he kept her around even as he knew he'd never get rid of her.

Ella tilted her head and smiled up at him.

70

Despite the audience, he couldn't resist dropping a light kiss on her lips and tasted the sweetness of the strawberry jam she'd eaten. He immediately regretted his hasty act for his body responded in a most obvious way. It didn't go unnoticed. Ella's eyes widened. Apparently her invisible friends took note as well for the pots hanging on the rack above the counter rattled in warning.

Zane sighed, a sound Ella echoed.

Reluctantly, he let her go, but he did twine his fingers around hers, knowing that even that simple touch would keep her voices at bay.

"Where are we going?" she asked with a sweet smile that made Zane want to throw her over his shoulder and carry her back to his room. He knew she wouldn't protest and the migraine and bruises from the missiles would pale in comparison to the pleasure he knew awaited. But he needed to find out if his theory held merit.

"I want you to meet an acquaintance of mine."

"Sure," she agreed readily. "Does this have to do with my voices? Because I'll have you know I've tried every drug there is out there with no effect. The best they ever achieved was a drooling state where I couldn't even argue with them. You're the only thing that's ever stopped them cold."

"Not all things can be cured with pills and I have access to resources humans don't."

"Like what?"

"Wait and see," he answered mysteriously. "Now, why don't you get changed into something a little more glamorous while I have some dinner?"

Ella brow furrowed. "Dinner? Oh, do you

mean you're going to bite somebody?"

Hendricks snorted.

Taken aback at her easy acceptance of something that made most humans cringe, he stammered a reply. "Er, yes. I'll be back shortly."

Zane wondered at the look of disappointment on her face as he called for someone from his stay at home menu. All vamps kept a few sheep around for when they didn't have time to hunt. In return, he took good care of them.

But even as he drank from Cherise, after sternly warning her not to play with him like he usually allowed, he wished it was another neck he sank his teeth into. How quickly she'd drawn him under her spell. Would the effect last once he got past the poltergeists protecting her? Would the thrill and her novelty wear off once he got a taste?

Only one way to find out. But first he needed to solve the dilemma plaguing his crazy little Ella.

Chapter Fifteen

Despite her happiness at seeing Zane, as soon as he strode away in search of his own dinner, reality sank in. He'd told her to change into something more glamorous for their outing. Given Ella wore the fanciest clothing she'd owned since a child, she wasn't quite sure how to accomplish that.

"What's wrong, little lamb?"

She fidgeted, afraid to admit her dilemma.

Lucky for her, Anna caught on. "Do you need help getting ready for your excursion with the master?"

She nodded.

"Never fear, little lamb. I'll make sure you sparkle. Come with me and let's see what we can find."

It seemed Hendricks hadn't just bought her the clothes she wore, but a wardrobe full. Dresses of varying styles and shades crammed a closet adjoining Zane's room. When Ella gaped at them, too overwhelmed by the myriad choices, Anna took over, holding up several styles before settling on a simple sheathe in a pale blue which fell to her knees and hugged her slim curves. The cook, turned stylist, had Ella sit so she could coif her hair. As the minutes dragged on and Zane didn't return Ella couldn't help but ask, "Where does he find people to bite?"

Anna didn't pause in her task but continued

to curl and coil Ella's hair, another new experience for Ella who'd only ever washed and brushed it.

"He keeps a few willing folk around for eating, but usually he prefers to hunt and keep his menu varied."

"Oh." Ella quieted as an unfamiliar feeling suffused her. She didn't like the idea of Zane biting but not because his diet repulsed her. Zane had to eat. Whether he drank from humans or ate a steak which was once a living cow, it didn't matter to her. What bothered her was how he did it. And with who. She couldn't help but imagine his lips touching skin, possibly another woman's. Making her sigh in pleasure. Holding his chosen one in his embrace, cradling her in the same arms which held her. Her agitation, and jealousy, made the voices in her head churn and she heard Anna gasp, probably because all the loose objects in the room rattled and a cool breeze wafted through the room.

As soon as Ella realized she'd riled her attic friends up, she clamped down on her mind and the brush, eye shadow and mascara floating above the vanity dropped with a clatter.

"Goodness!" Anna exclaimed.

Ella couldn't help but curl her shoulders, chagrin setting in over frightening the woman who'd been so kind to help her. "Sorry Anna. Sometimes the voices in my head get a little hyper."

"Well, that little display certainly explains the master's bedroom."

Ella blushed. "Sorry about that. Zane kissed me and they didn't like that."

Anna chuckled. "No wonder the master seemed so pleased with himself. Kisses powerful enough to create a tornado."

"More like target practice," Ella admitted. "And right when things were getting interesting."

"We can't have that now, can we. Never fear, little lamb, I'm sure the master will find a way to get those voices to behave. Now, take a look in the mirror and tell me what you think. It's not perfect, but it will do for the night and as soon as we can arrange it, we'll have a hairdresser come to the house and style your hair."

Pivoting on the stool, Ella turned to peer in the mirror and lost her breath, because staring back at her was a princess. "Who is that?" she asked.

"The most beautiful woman to grace this house," said Zane coming up behind her and resting his hands on her shoulders that peeked out daringly from the top of a gown that bared too much white skin.

Ella couldn't turn from the vision in the mirror, entranced with the smoky eyes, coiled hair with wisping tendrils and pink rosebud lips. On some level she realized it was her, but a version of herself she'd never imagined.

Tears pricked her eyes and she found herself pivoted on the seat with Zane dropping to his knees in front of her. "Why do you cry?"

"Oh Zane, you've been so wonderful to me. What if this is all a dream? I'm a crazy girl. Things like this don't happen to people like me. I'm afraid of waking up."

Gentle fingers brushed at her lashes, wiping the tears before they could leak free. He leaned close, pressing his lips to hers softly. "Welcome to your new life, Ella. This is only the beginning."

Lacing her fingers into his, stilling the voices which exhorted her not to fall under the devil's spell, he helped her stand and with a dashing smile, took her to meet his mysterious friend.

Ella didn't care where she went. *So long as he's with me, I'd follow him anywhere.*

Chapter Sixteen

Completely beguiled, that was what Zane found himself. His sweet Ella attracted him before with her pretty looks, her waifish style attractive in a match girl kind of way. However now, with her hair elegantly coiffed, a light application of makeup, and a gown that showcased her slender, yet shapely figure, she was breathtaking.

It took quite a bit of will power not to bury his face in the smooth expanse of her exposed neck, and a moment's trepidation flashed through him at the thought of where he planned to take her. Perhaps he should have dressed her like a nun, but the hiding of her neck would have been an insult. A slap in the face to the one he went to for aid that said 'I don't trust you'. Of course, he didn't trust anybody, not even himself at times, but the fact remained, in order to play the games that his kind indulged in out of boredom, he had to put Ella at risk.

It would have been better if he'd had the opportunity to place his mark on her the night before. Then again, his inability to do so was what led on their current outing.

Damn. I only met her a few days ago and already my life is so much more complicated. But complicated or not, he would change nothing, the anticipation that coursed through his body more addictive than any human drug. *For the first time since my turning, I am alive.*

"Where are we going?" Ella asked, once he'd seated her next to him in his convertible.

"We are off to see an acquaintance of mine who may be able to shed some light on your voices."

"Another vampire?" She asked this with the wide eyed excitement of a child inquiring of Santa, her naivety endearing, but oh so dangerous. Where he took her, they ate, quite literally, innocents such as her. He'd have to guard her closely.

"Yes, she is a vampire. Actually there are bound to be quite a few of my kind in attendance. And they won't be the only legendary beings you will encounter. Quite a few fantastical people might be present. Please, keep in mind though, that no matter how benign many of them might appear, you must treat them with caution. Not all of them will treat you with the same courtesy as I. You must promise to stay close to me and not speak to anyone."

"I'll be glued to your side," she solemnly promised. "Is there anything else I should know so I don't offend anyone? As you might have guessed, I've never really attended any events or gatherings, unless social time at the asylum counts. I hardly think my ability to paint by number or play tic tac toe is going to come in handy."

He laughed. "No, the games those present play will be more subtle than that, and dangerous. We enter a world where politics, relationships and perceived slights can start feuds. Where even a smile or frown at the wrong person can lead to misunderstanding and bloodshed."

"And you think going is a good idea?"

"No. But, the person we need to speak to will be there."

"Couldn't we just have called?"

He arched a brow and shot her a crooked grin. "Now where would the fun be in doing that?"

"You're trying to take your friend by surprise."

"Yes." No point in denying it. They'd long enjoyed a see saw type of power rivalry, a friendly one of course, to help pass the centuries. "But back to your earlier query of what you should do. Try not to look anyone in the eye. Many of those present will have the ability to beguile humans. You won't even realize it is happening."

"Is this like the sleep thing you tried to do to me? The one that didn't work." An impish smile graced her lips and mirth danced in her eyes.

How delectable she appeared. Zane almost pulled the car over, the desire to kiss her almost overpowering. His lust, barely in check since he'd beheld her in her finery, protested when he did nothing. He focused on her reminder of his ignoble failure to spell her. "Yes, just like that," he grumbled.

Ella giggled. "I think someone is still upset his little spell didn't work."

"This is no laughing matter, moonbeam. Some of the beings, such as the elves and fairies, and even some of the older vamps, are stronger than I and might take you unaware. I'd rather not test and see if you are immune to everyone."

"What did you call me?" Her laughter halted mid giggle and her regard turned serious.

"I called you moonbeam because you have the same beauty and glow."

"Oh."

Tears brimmed on her lashes, and for a moment he wondered at their cause. Then, like a sucker punch to the gut, he understood. She'd probably never had a nickname, or at least not an affectionate one. How the knowledge made his ancient heart ache—and his rage against those who'd done her wrong simmer, demanding vengeance. Instead of hunting down all those who'd treated her ill, he decided to bring back her smile. Tears and vulnerability would get her eaten alive where they were going. "Moonbeam also suits you perfectly because you make me want to get naked and dance in your light and dodge the rocks your friends are sure to fire my way."

Silvery bells rang out as she laughed, just as he'd intended. Reaching out to twine his fingers around hers, he didn't know if he should curse or rejoice at the way she kept drawing out the humanity he'd thought lost forever. But at the same time, she also roused the possessive beast, one which already looked upon her as his own and woe to anyone who thought to hurt her in any way.

Chapter Seventeen

Good grief. The grandeur of their destination took her by surprise. Ella gawked at the mansion they stood in front of. She'd thought Zane's place grand, but this...this was insane. She clung tightly to Zane's hand. *I don't know if this was a good idea.* She was so out of her element. He smiled down at her reassuringly and she held in a sigh. She might not belong in this world, but for him, she'd try.

Striding up to the massive metal embossed doors, she tried not to trip in the slipper-like shoes Anna had found for her. They'd vetoed heels since Ella had never walked in a pair and they'd both feared she'd twist an ankle.

The double doors swung open at their approach and Zane didn't pause at the entrance, just strode into the well-lit vestibule that gaped around and above them. People milled around, elegantly dressed, talking and smiling, but something about them made Ella shiver. A sense of otherness emanated from them and she caught more than one flash of canine and in one case, ruby red eyes as Zane strode through their ranks headed for a specific destination.

Okay, maybe not people after all. And unlike Zane who makes me feel safe, these folk make me wish I were huddled back in the safety of the institute. She'd have to be crazy to not realize some of these beings were dangerous. *I am so out of my element.* She didn't belong here. No human did.

Head ducked so as to not inadvertently meet anyone's gaze, Ella held tight to Zane's hand. She trusted him to keep her safe, but if these beings, wearing thin veneers of humanity came at them all at once, it didn't take her voices humming in displeasure for her to know it would get ugly.

If she'd found that the crowd milling about the front entrance gave her the creeps, it was nothing compared to the chill that went down her spine when they entered the lavish ballroom. Imagine, a vast auditorium-like space, times ten, with the ceiling soaring so high, she would have had to tilt her head at an unnatural angle to see above her. Gilded gold columns ringed the room, twined in greenery and lit with twinkling little lights. The floor underneath was a black shiny stone like substance, *"Marble",* murmured a brave voice. But the opulent room was nothing compared to the people occupying it.

Zane hadn't exaggerated when he'd mentioned she would encounter fantastical personages. Fluttery wings projected from the back of a silver haired maiden, horns from the forehead of a brutish other. Skin hues from the palest ivory to the deepest ebony, to colors never before seen— blue, green and even pink—speckled the crowd. And yet, in the face of all this evident supernaturalness, a hush fell over the ensemble at their entrance. Ella couldn't help the heat that rose to her cheeks as dozens of pairs of eyes swung to peruse them, judge them. Even though she held Zane's hand in a grip meant to crush bone, one of the voices in her mind dared whisper, *"Danger. Danger. Oh dear child, what have you done?"*

What indeed? But there was no halting her vampire on a mission. Head held high, not deigning to address the curiosity aimed their way, he strode across the room as if he owned it. Fearless, and she could only scurry at his side, eyes down, focused on her feet. Only when Zane stopped his steady march did Ella raise her eyes to see a dais. Several steps above the floor, in a white polished marble, the platform held an ornate throne, like something out of medieval times, and perched on the golden chair, sat pure power encased in the form of a young girl.

How did she know that? Probably because all the voices in her head screamed at once. It was all she could do not to wince. Ella moved closer to Zane, not understanding why this slip of a girl frightened her and her friends in the attic. She didn't look mighty, but Ella knew without a shadow of a doubt that she was the most dangerous thing in the room. *And we've come to see her.* How not reassuring.

"Zane," said the girl in dulcet tones. "I see you've brought me a gift."

"Not quite, Felicia," Zane said stiffly, his fingers tightening around Ella's in silent warning. "I've come to ask for your expertise in a matter."

"What? The mighty Zane asking for help? I'm shocked," replied Felicia with a titter. She rose from her throne and took dainty steps down the dais until she stood in front of Ella. Eyes of pure black peered at her and Ella held tight to her bladder, fear coursing through her. "Oh my. I can see why you've come. It will cost you."

A heavy sigh left Zane. "It always does."

"I assume you'd rather we not do this in front of my court?"

"If you don't mind. I'd prefer we discuss this affair in private."

"Very well" With swinging hips, Felicia led them around the platform to an entrance hidden behind a heavy tapestry. A man stood guard and he opened the door, never taking his yellow slitted eyes from Ella. She shivered at the coldness they emitted. Not quite human, and definitely unafraid to use the giant axe, held in readiness by his side. For some reason, she thought of Alice, the one who went down the rabbit hole and wondered how many times Felicia had shouted to her guard, "Off with their head!" Somehow she doubted she'd like the number.

They entered a large office with wall to wall bookcases filled with books and, if Ella's eyes didn't deceive her, scrolls. How fascinating.

Zane seated Ella in an armchair covered in soft leather, while he perched on the arm rest, his long fingers resting lightly on her neck keeping her wailing voices mostly at bay.

The door slid shut and Felicia dropped her seductive pose as she leaned against her desk, facing them. "Where on earth did you find this prize, Zane? I haven't seen her ilk in a long time."

"Her name is Ella. I found her in a mental institution. We're here because I wanted your opinion on a problem plaguing her. See, Ella hears voices and they *do* things."

"I'll bet they do," murmured Felicia. "Move away from her Zane. I will not hurt your protégé, but your very nearness prevents me from fully seeing what I sense she is."

Ella wanted to protest and ask Zane to stay close to her, however she couldn't say anything, too intimidated by Felicia. She also didn't want to offend her. Ella might not understand what was going on, but Zane seemed to think this Felicia person could help with the voices.

With a brush of his fingers on her cheek, and a murmured, "Fear not, you will not come to harm," he moved away.

Immediately her friends upstairs filled the silent void in her mind. They whispered and gibbered incoherently, their fear palpable.

"Gawd almighty, now you've gone and done it."

"We're all going to die!"

"Fee, Fi, Fo Fum, I smell a vampire and she's going to kill us for fun."

Ella paid them no mind. It didn't take a genius to realize she sat before someone dangerous.

"Look at me, child."

But Ella remembered Zane's instructions and stared at her knotted fingers.

"It's alright, moonbeam. Do as she says."

Darting him a look, Ella caught his reassuring smile. If he thought she should then...

Her gaze rose until it met Felicia's dark ones which dilated. Ella found herself drawn into those bottomless depths and the voices keened and babbled in her mind. Several thumps and an unladylike curse later and Ella found herself released from whatever spell Felicia had put her under. Dizzy and unsure of what just happened, Ella hugged her arms around her upper body in an attempt to calm herself and in turn the voices, which in their frenzy had pulled books and scrolls from the walls. The impromptu missiles hovered in the air menacingly.

Irritation marked Felicia's face. "I might remind you she came to me." A book sailed at her narrowly missing her head and Ella realized that Felicia spoke to the voices, not her or Zane. Did that make her crazy too? Felicia's face tightened. "I mean her no harm, so stop before I forget my promise of aid and instead do what you so fear of our kind. You know I don't threaten lightly."

Instantly the voices quieted and the levitating objects dropped to the floor in a thumping rain.

Ella let out a breath she hadn't realized she'd been holding. "I'm sorry. The voices get violent if they think I'm threatened."

"They are just protecting you, which in turn protects them."

"I don't know about that. They're usually the reason I get into trouble and why I've spent most of my life in institutions." Ella couldn't help but reply with a bitterness accrued from years of mistreatment.

"You manifested special powers and yet the doctors thought you were crazy? Idiots," Felicia mumbled shaking her head. "But no more than I expect from the close minded. I must ask, how many voices do you hear Ella?"

"I don't know. A lot. I tried counting once, but after the first two hundred, I gave up."

Her words took Felicia aback. "By the dark one. Zane, you've found yourself a mighty prize. I don't suppose you'd reconsider giving her up. I'd reward you handsomely."

"She's mine." He growled the possessive words and Ella smiled at him even though what she really wanted to do was throw herself in his arms and kiss him. She'd wait until they got out of here for that. As if sensing her need for him, Zane returned to his previous position, seating himself on the arm of the chair, his hand once again draped possessively on her nape, silence the gibbering masses. "So I was right. Ella isn't mad."

"I'm not?"

"Not at all, dear child."

"Care to tell us? You still haven't told us what she is." Zane queried.

"You mean you don't know?"

"Would I ask if I did?"

Felicia shook her head. "Sometimes I forget you forewent training in the arcane arts. Although, even if you had you might not have guessed it. Ella is a rarity that few know about. She is an *ánima veneficus*.

"In English, please."

"She's a soul sorceress."

Ella's brow creased. "I'm a witch?"

"Bah, nothing so crude or petty as that. You, my dear, are a very rare soul sorceress, capable of mighty feats of magic."

"You must be mistaken."

"I am never mistaken," was Felicia's dry reply.

"Then I don't understand. I hear voices, they throw things, how does that make me a sorceress?"

"The voices you hear, they are the souls that have attached themselves to you, drawn by your innate ability to see them even in death."

"You mean," Ella whispered. "I hear dead people." Then she laughed. "Oh, that's funny. You think I'm psychic."

Felicia sighed loudly. "Zane, would you make your protégé understand this is no joke."

Ella craned to peek at Zane. "Surely you don't believe that. I mean, seriously, who hears ghosts?"

"You do." He dropped to his knees alongside her and clasped her hands. "Ella, listen to what Felicia says. If she says you hear the voices of the departed, then you do. You have to admit, it makes sense. It explains their knowledge and the way they can move things."

"So I'm haunted. How is that any better than being crazy?"

"If the voices are souls, and you have the power to hear them, then I'll bet that means you can find a way to control them. Think of it, Ella. If you can develop your power to keep them behaved, then you can have peace even when I'm not around."

"But I like having you around." She could tell her simple declaration pleased him because a soft smile graced his lips.

"And I enjoy having you around too. But I'd prefer to do so without having to worry about injury." He stroked the inside of her palm, his dark eyes filled with a seductive promise which sent a shiver down her spine.

Oh, to be able to indulge in the heat his gaze promised. She turned her attention to the avidly watching Felicia. "Can you make them go away?" Ella held her breath as she waited for a reply.

"No, I doubt anyone can. And why would you want to? You are powerful, child, more powerful than you can imagine, and if your benefactor were anybody but my old friend Zane, I would either capture you for my use or kill you."

"So I'm stuck with them. Great. Now instead of just being Crazy Ella, I can be Crazy Ghost Lady Ella. Nothing changes for me. I get to spend the rest of my life hearing dead people, and having them ruin everything positive that ever comes my way."

"Only if you let them. Silly girl. Up until now, you've allowed them free rein. That has to stop. You need to learn how to control them. From the sounds of it, they attached themselves to you young, a hard thing I'm sure especially with no one to teach you. But you are a woman grown now. It is time you took control. Reminded these spirits that you are the one in charge. That they obey you."

Felicia made it sound so easy. "And if they don't listen?" Ella had been trying all her life to make the voices shut up, and look where it had gotten her.

"Until you learn how to control them yourself, use Zane to keep them in line."

"What do you mean?" he asked. "The damned things tried to give me a concussion."

Felicia scoffed. "They panicked and you forget who you are *vampire*. Or do you think we earned the title 'drinker of souls' for nothing?"

Ella looked up at Zane who bore a thoughtful expression on his face. "I'd forgotten about that aspect of our curse. I haven't drained a human since I was first turned."

The feeling of missing something had Ella waving a hand and interrupting. "Um, do you guys mind explaining to the human over here? What are you talking about?"

Felicia chuckled and it wasn't exactly a pretty sound. Ella shivered.

"Ah dear child, you have so much to learn. But here's the part you need to know. When a vampire completely drains a human, he can also ingest the soul. It used to be a common practice until our kind realized that the spirits we took in became a part of us, permanently. The clashing psyches can often be quite alarming. Some vampires have even gone insane. To halt the descent into madness, we now tend to sip from multiple humans instead of sucking them dry. It's much healthier for our sanity and it also makes us less noticeable to human society."

"Okay, I guess I understand that, but how can Zane help me with the ghosts in my head? It's not like they have bodies he can suck dry to get rid of them."

"Aah but that's just it, you are the body for the souls. If they refuse to listen, then simply let him feed on you. As he feeds, he can draw on his vampiric abilities and siphon spirits from you. Of course if he takes in too many of them he may go insane, but he can rid you of quite a few spirits before that happens."

"But I don't want him to go crazy. I'd rather keep the voices then."

Felicia rolled her eyes. "Humans are so emotional. I didn't say he had to, just that he could if the voices refused to obey. Warn them to toe the line and listen, else you'll sic Zane on them. And you'll only need to use that threat until you learn how to control them yourself. You have the power to do so. Practice will hone that skill and open up other powerful avenues you never imagined."

To find out she wasn't nuts just possessed, okay maybe it wasn't yet an improvement, but it sounded like she had a possibility of gaining control of her mind and life. "But how will I learn?" Ella looked at Felicia beseechingly.

Felicia sighed. "Damn Zane, I am not into girls, but even I can feel her pull. I will help you, but, for this you will owe me a favor."

"Done," said Zane.

"I wasn't talking to you," said Felicia slyly. "I want a favor from Ella."

"Sure," she said.

"Ella, don't be so quick to say yes. You don't know yet what she wants of you," Zane interjected, concern lacing his voice.

Ella tilted her face towards Zane's. "All my life I was thought insane. For the first time I have the chance to be normal. Well, almost normal. I don't care what she wants. So long as it's not you, I don't care." Ella turned to face Felicia. "What do you want from me?"

Felicia smiled in triumph. "I'm not sure yet. Consider it a favor owed. One day I will collect upon it. Now, I really should get back to my guests. Zane, you will bring her back tomorrow night when things are quieter and I will begin her lessons. In the meantime, if the spirits continue to give you trouble when indulging in certain delicate past-times, just remember what I said about threatening them."

With a throaty laugh, Felicia left them.

Ella stood and threw herself into Zane's arms. "I'm not crazy."

"Oh, I don't know about that. You are hanging out with a vampire voluntarily," he teased.

Ella giggled, feeling more carefree than she could remember. Zane's arms tightened around her and she tilted her face up towards him in time for the kiss.

And what a kiss.

Hard lips slanted over hers, their electric touch sending a jolt through her body, one that set her heart racing and made wetness pool between her thighs. She clutched at his shoulders, unsure if her legs would hold her. She needn't have feared. He wouldn't let her fall.

His hands cupped her bottom through her silky gown and he pressed her against him, his erection evident against her lower belly.

"My sweet, and now powerful moonbeam," he said when he let her come up for air and she wondered-*Do vampires have to breathe?* "You make me forget where we are when I touch you. Come, we should leave this place while the night is still young."

A befuddled Ella followed when he led her by the hand through the crowd that still filled the ballroom.

The room seemed more packed than when they'd entered, the energy and wildness more palpable, as was the danger. Zane forged through the press of beings who moved out of his way, their curious eyes flicking from him to her. As instructed, Ella didn't let her gaze touch anyone else's, but that didn't stop someone from snagging her around the waist, ripping her hand free from Zane's grasp.

Startled, she peered up and only got a brief impression of dark skin and possibly horns. She didn't have time to scream or wonder before she found herself freed from the creatures grip and tucked behind Zane's rigid back.

"You dare touch what is mine?" A Zane she barely recognized spoke to the creature in a cold, controlled tone.

The demon—because she knew not what else it could be—had obviously been drinking too much because he laughed. Not a really good idea judging by the anger that radiated from Zane's whole body.

Quicker than lightning striking, the demon ended flat on the floor, his head tilted at an odd angle and his eyes unseeing. Ella held her breath in shock, while her friends upstairs cheered Zane's action. Apparently, he'd finally done something they approved of.

The ballroom went silent and the press of bodies moved back from them, leaving them in a cleared circle.

A part of Ella knew she should be horrified. Zane had killed someone for just touching her. But, and she might burn in hell for thinking this, she thought it was the nicest thing anyone had ever done for her. In a perverted way, she also found it romantic. She finally had someone who wanted to protect her. *My very own vampire in dark armor.*

Chapter Eighteen

How dare someone lay hands on her! Rage permeated his body as Zane pivoted on one heel in a circle to assess their level of danger. He glared at the crowd and his lip curled back in a snarl. "Anyone else want to touch what is mine?" he demanded, unable to stem his irrational anger.

No one answered, although a few shook their heads and retreated further.

The crowd parted and Felicia stepped into view. "I believe you've made your point," she said dryly. Turning to the guard who'd followed she said, "Felix, clean up this mess." She turned back to them and shook her head at Zane as if he were a naughty child. "If you're done killing my guests, I shall see you and your woman on the morrow."

Her words started up the buzz of conversation again although the space around Zane and Ella remained clear. No longer able to delay the inevitable, Zane turned to face Ella, resigned to see the horror etched on her face as she realized she had put her faith and trust in a monster.

It was even worse than he'd expected. He groaned when he saw her. Her eyes shone brightly, but not with tears. She appeared happy. Smiling, she leaned up on tiptoe and kissed him, a chaste kiss that nevertheless made him hard. "Thank you," she murmured.

Shaking his head at his own jealousy and her

even odder acceptance of it, he took them back out into the night before he started killing the crowd for even looking at Ella. *My moonbeam.*

Once seated in the car, he turned to her before starting the engine, a crease on his brow. "Why are you not horrified by what I did?" It made so sense. Humans, especially women, cringed in the face of violent death.

"Because you care." She leaned forward and gave him another butterfly kiss that made him want to take her in the car, bucket seats be damned.

"But I killed him."

Ella shrugged. "Are you going to tell me that thing was a boy scout? That if you hadn't been around he wouldn't have tried to hurt me?" When he just looked at her in disbelief, she smiled. "I'm not like other girls, Zane. My years in the hospital taught me that in order to not get stepped on, I had to be the baddest of the bunch. Or in my case, the craziest. If people fear you, then no one is stupid enough to mess with you. That means doing things that aren't always nice. My voices used to set the stage by levitating and throwing stuff. Their shenanigans are how I remained a virgin and virtually untouched, unlike a lot of the other patients. Is killing a little extreme? In my world maybe, but I'd say in your world, nothing short of death will gain you the respect you need to stay alive."

Innocent, naïve, but at the same time, wiser than many. What a contradiction she could be. Another one of her many charms, and yet one more reason why he wanted her with a passion that should have frightened him.

Aroused and still somewhat enraged at the temerity of the demon, he decided he needed to calm down before he took her home and unleashed his passion on her. Seeing a Dairy Queen with the lights still on, he pulled in.

"Why are we stopping?" she asked.

"Ever had a sundae?" he asked, holding the restaurant door open for her so she could precede him.

"Isn't that something with ice cream?" she asked, craning to look around with interest.

Her words touched a sad chord in him. Even vampires who had no need of human food knew the taste of a sundae. Deprived of so many things, Zane intended to introduce Ella to the pleasures she'd missed out on, starting with a decadent treat.

Zane ordered for her—a true banana split with caramel and cherries to top it. They sat facing each other at the back of the restaurant in the hard plastic booth.

Ella looked at the sugary concoction warily, but after the first spoonful, she closed her eyes and groaned. "Oh my," she said when she finally opened her eyes. "That is heavenly."

Judging by her moans and smiles, she found the icy treat pleasurable, but Zane watching her obvious enjoyment thought she was the true pleasure. When she licked the spoon, her pink tongue darting out to suck the melting cream, he grew rock hard.

"Let me taste," he growled.

Chagrined, she showed him the empty bowl. "I'm sorry. I ate it all."

"That's okay, that's not where I want to taste it." He leaned across the table and cupping her head to draw her forward, claimed her mouth.

She gasped when he licked her lips, the sugar from her dessert still not as tasty as her blood, but definitely arousing.

"Let's go home." Holding her hand, he led her back to the car. He took the roads leading home fast. The smell of her arousal filled the car, causing the most painful of erections.

Never had a woman affected him so. Made him lose control. Even more amazing, she seemed to share this irrational desire.

When they reached the house, he parked out front and in a flash, had her out of the car. Too impatient to wait, he swung her into his arms and strode up the steps to the door. As if he'd spent the evening waiting for this moment, Hendricks swung the door open as he reached the house.

"Hi," chirped Ella, even as she blushed a becoming pink.

"Evening Master, Milady," said Hendricks, who couldn't hide the twinkle in his eye.

But Zane didn't care if his servant thought him foolish, the feel and scent of his moonbeam had driven all the reason from his mind. He only knew he wanted her. Now. Naked in his arms. Crying out his name.

He took the stairs two at a time, cursing the fact his bedroom lay in the furthest corner of the house.

When he dropped her onto the bed, she giggled, then frowned.

"Go away. You heard what the lady vampire

said. He'll eat you."

Zane didn't want her distracted by the dratted voices. Palming her ankle, he pulled her towards him on the satiny coverlet and she gasped. He removed her shoes and placed a hand on each of her legs, sliding his hands up her silky, smooth skin.

"Have they shut up or do I also need to warn them?" Zane would suck in a thousand souls at this moment if that was what it took to claim her.

"They're gone for now." She held out her arms, an invitation he could not refuse. First though, he stripped, removing his jacket and impatient, ripping the buttons from his shirt as he peeled it off.

Ella licked her lips and watched him, her lids heavy with building passion.

Zane undid the button on his pants, but kept them on. A part of him urged caution lest he overwhelm her. Ready and no longer willing to wait, he crawled onto the bed between her legs, legs which she spread to accommodate him, the skirt of her gown riding up.

Bracing himself on his arms, he leaned over her and found her lips again. They kissed with a frantic passion, her fingers twining and pulling at his hair, while he nudged his erection, still covered by his trousers, against the apex of her thighs. She arched back against him, her gasps and moans, nearly shredding what little control he had.

Time and again, he had to remind himself of her virgin state because his impulse was to push up her dress, rip off her panties and plunge into the wet core that he knew ached for him.

Dragging his lips from hers, he nibbled his way to her neck, kissing the pulsing vein that fluttered under her fine skin. The chill breeze that swept over him, made him move down. There was no need to antagonize the voices. They seemed willing so far to allow them to take their pleasure. The biting could come later.

Her dress stopped his exploration of her breasts. Unacceptable. Tearing the fabric with his teeth, he rent the satiny material, baring her beautiful tits.

The first swirl of his tongue on her nipple had her arching and crying out. Zane grinned in masculine pride and took the pointed nub into his mouth, sucking. She whimpered, her pleasure quite vocal, and he sucked harder.

"Tell me how it feels?" he asked gruffly when he switched his attention to her other nipple.

"Like I'm on fire," she whispered. "Oh please. I want. . ."

"What do you want?" he asked pausing to look at her. She appeared so beautiful with her face flushed and her eyes glazed in passion.

"I don't know what I want. Zane. Please." She begged and Zane almost came like an untried youth at her need.

He slid his hand up her thigh, smooth silky skin, her skin. His fingers encountered the scrap of material that covered her mound and he tore it off, exposing her to him. He stroked her curls, soft caresses that had her writhing. But her desire called him. Her scent entranced him. His digit delved between her thighs and touched her between her slick folds.

She screamed.

He stroked her again and she shuddered.

Zane slid down her body until he could see her pink flesh. The musky scent of her arousal teased and beckoned him. Placing his hands under her buttocks, he pulled her up to his mouth and tasted her.

Sweet heaven.

At the first touch of his tongue, she came, crying out and trembling in his grasp. But Zane had just started. He parted her moist lips with his tongue and lapped at her, the nectar from her sex energizing him. He found her clit and sucked it, digging his fingers into the soft skin of her buttocks as she bucked and cried out, lost in a mindless maelstrom of pleasure.

Zane could have eaten from her all day, she tasted so good, but he knew if he didn't take her now, he'd embarrass himself. Sliding a finger into her sex, he groaned at the tightness of her sheath even as he used his other hand to pull down his trousers.

And that's when the objects started to fly.

Chapter Nineteen

Amidst the fuzzy pleasure that clouded her mind, Ella heard Zane curse and the wondrous things he did to her body stopped.

She opened her eyes with difficulty and blinked. Then cursed.

"You've got to be kidding me," she grumbled, quickly losing her pleasurable glow as she saw Zane, his pants gaping, under attack. "Stop it," she shouted. But the voices wailed in her head about keeping her pure and not letting the vampire desecrate her. Ella almost rolled her eyes. So licking her private parts was okay, but actual penetration wasn't? Stupid ghostly semantics.

Hopping off the bed, she protected Zane the only way she could think of, by covering his body with her own. She wrapped herself around him, or tried to. The man did tower over her, but her shield ploy worked. The aerial attack stopped.

"I'm sorry," she mumbled against his chest.

Cool fingers titled her chin up and Zane smiled down at her ruefully. "We've learned your friends have limits. Apparently, your virginity is one of them."

"No fair. It's my body."

Zane hugged her tight. "Soon, my impatient moonbeam. Felicia will teach you what you need to know and no longer will the voices act on your unwilling behalf."

"It can't be soon enough," she grumbled. "Why didn't you just bite me and suck one of them out? Felicia said that might work."

"This is going to sound stupidly sentimental and human, but I felt your first time should be real. The bite makes anything pleasurable. I want your experience to be memorable because you feel and want it."

A surge of affection, dare she even say love, rushed through her and she hugged him tightly. *And he thinks he's a monster. Boy is he wrong. I've met monsters. He's a knight in shining armor compared to them.*

With dawn approaching, he led them back to the bed. Ella paused to shrug off the shredded remains of her dress. She'd lost her modesty a long time ago, but she blushed at the heated look on his face. Naked, she crawled into bed with him. Zane, for his part still wore his unbuttoned trousers.

She snuggled up to him, her hand on the naked skin of his chest, stroking him softly and thinking about the unbelievably pleasurable things he'd done to her before the rude interruption.

While he'd sated some of her curiosity and passion, she still craved. Craved Zane. She wanted to give him pleasure too, she just wasn't sure how to go about it. The occasional furtive glimpses she'd seen in the hospital not exactly a step by step manual for seduction. She decided to try and mimic some of the things he'd done to her. Leaning up, she placed her mouth on his flat nipple.

"What are you doing, moonbeam?" he growled.

"I want to please you."

"You don't have to do this. I can wait."

"But I want to," she said nipping him. His groan started the fire in her again and she enjoyed herself toying with his nipples. However, what she truly wanted to see and feel lay lower.

Straddling his thighs, she parted his slacks and gasped at the sight of his erection jutting from the top of his briefs.

"Goodness. And this is supposed to fit?"

"Like a key in a lock."

"If you say so." She reached out and ran a finger down his length. His shaft jumped and she pulled her hand back.

"It moved!"

"Because I liked it."

"I only touched you."

"Do it again," he groaned.

Tugging his briefs and slacks down with his help, she bared him completely. *Oh my god.* Long and thick, his cock seemed to pulse. Ella reached out a tentative hand and rubbed the swollen tip of his penis. Again, his dick twitched, but she was ready for it this time and didn't shy away. She kept touching him and a pearl of liquid appeared at the tip.

Emboldened, she wrapped a hand around him and his shaft jerked like a living beast. But she held on.

Zane moaned. She looked up to see his eyes closed and his face clenched tight as if in agony.

"Am I doing this wrong?"

Jaw clenched tight, he managed to utter through gritted teeth. "No. Too right. I fear I shan't last long if you keep it up."

Really? Feeling braver, she decided to try

something even bolder. Leaning down, the ends of her hair brushing his groin, she licked the tip of his mushroom head, tasting the glistening drop. Zane sucked in a harsh breathe.

Pleased at his reaction and determined to do more, she took him in her mouth, unsure but willing to experiment.

"Holy fuck, moonbeam!" Zane shouted at her hoarsely, his hips bucking. Excitement coursed through her. She liked having Zane out of control. She sucked him awkwardly at first, but she quickly found a rhythm and method that had him thrashing and clawing at the sheets. How powerful she felt in that moment. And aroused.

"Turn around," he whispered in a hoarse voice. "Let me lick you at the same time."

Ella shuddered and moisture pooled between her legs. Shifting positions, too titillated to feel embarrassed about this new intimate position, she positioned her moist sex over his face.

She latched her mouth around his cock again even as his mouth found her core and licked. He gripped her by the buttocks, his tongue flicking and sucking at her, and when her pelvic muscles clenched and spasmed in an orgasm that had her screaming around the thick head in her mouth, he came finally in a hot jet that she swallowed eagerly.

Loose limbed and sated, she collapsed on him, her face on his muscled thigh. Gentle hands tugged at her until she lay snuggled at his side, wrapped in his arms.

The whirring sound of the shutters closing signaled the arrival of the dawn. But Ella was already asleep in her dark prince's arms.

Chapter Twenty

It gave him more pleasure than he could have explained to awake and find Ella still cuddled with him, her silvery blonde hair draped across his chest, along with half of her naked body.

Tenderness, an alien emotion for him since the change, filled him as he stroked the silken skin of her back. He'd known his little moonbeam such a short time and yet, already he couldn't imagine life, or in his case un-life, without her.

She continually surprised him, and not just with her seduction of him the night before which had surpassed every sexual encounter he'd had in his long life. He loved the fact that she accepted him for what he was. Or had so far. She'd taken his violent and jealous nature in stride, even complimented him on it, but he'd disposed of the demon in a quick and tidy fashion. There were times when the violence that revolved around him because of who he was would erupt in a much more bloody fashion. Would she still find it sexy when she saw him for the first time rip the still beating heart from his enemy? Or when he tore open their flesh with his teeth, eschewing weapons for a more hands on, and dental, approach.

A part of him didn't want her to ever see that monster he'd become, but at the same time, he would not hide who he was. How he lived. Ignorance was danger.

And given what Felicia told him of Ella's power, he'd probably have more than his share of danger to face in order to keep her safe. Was it perverse of him to look forward to the challenge? Pitting himself against those who would dare try and steal his woman, his moonbeam, made his teeth ache for action and his adrenaline rise.

He would let no one hurt her. But while he could physically protect her, could he shield her from her own emotions? Ella had yet to experience or see how he fed. Ella was young, inexperienced and, if he weren't misreading her, falling in love with him. Jealousy was a big possibility. How would she react when she saw just how close he had to get to his dinner? Would she understand that the pleasure his victims took was not of his making but yet another aspect of his vampire heritage? Or would the thing he needed to remain alive be the act that finally toppled the pedestal she'd placed him on?

He didn't want to find out. Easing out from under her, he decided to feed now while she slept. Once he could be sure of her affections, then he'd let her see this final aspect of his cursed existence.

Or maybe he'd hide it from her forever so that he'd never have to see the disgust he feared. Or deal with the hurt in her eyes. He wasn't sure his newly discovered heart could handle that.

Chapter Twenty One

A whirring of the blinds as they rose woke her. Ella stretched and smiled. Her body tingled in the most intimate of places. Her skin felt so sensitized and aware. Even the slide of the silk sheets against her made her squirm. Last night, Zane had woken her body to pleasure and now it seemed, she wanted to indulge again and again.

Speaking of whom, where was Zane? She'd slept soundly and late judging by the deepening twilight sky she could out the windows.

"He's already moved on to greener pastures."

"You are nothing to him."

The voices yammered on and on, trying to plant doubt. She ignored them.

Showering quickly, rinsing her sticky body, she dressed in the new outfit she found lying on the freshly made bed when she exited the bathroom. Then she went to look for her lover.

He didn't appear to be in any of the main rooms so she wandered into the kitchen and found Anna along with a host of mouthwatering smells.

"There you are, lamb. The master said you'd waken soon. I'm just finishing up your food for you."

Perching herself on a chair, Ella took the proffered buttered roll and bit into the fresh, warm bread with a happy sigh. "Where is Zane?"

"Around," said Anna vaguely with a wave of

her spatula. "Why don't you go sit in the dining room and he'll join you shortly."

As vague answers went, Ella didn't like it. She had more than a sneaky suspicion about what Zane was doing and she wanted to roll her eyes at the obtuse way they were going about to make her ignore it. He was a vampire. He had to eat. So logic said he was feeding and the fact they were trying to hide it meant they thought she wouldn't appreciate seeing it.

Which means he's probably chomping on a girl. Not that the sex of his food source meant anything, but Ella remembered Zane telling her the bite was highly pleasurable. And that fact along with the continued whispers by the voices put her in a jealous rage.

There had only been one place she hadn't checked on the main floor during her wandering and Ella marched there now, the closed door only making her simmer more hotly.

The door swung open and hit the wall without her touching it and her hair waved around her head in a frantic dance as the voices chortled in her head.

"She's finally going to kill him."
"Stake the cheating bastard."
"Who wants popcorn?"

Ella strode in and stopped dead. Her jealous anger rose a notch as she saw Zane release the woman whose neck he sucked. He turned to face her, a look of horror on his face. It might have appeared comical were it not for the female he'd dropped like a hot potato. The brunette bimbo he'd fed on lolled on the couch, a look of rapture on her face.

Out of control, the voices acted on her behalf. They levitated the woman up from the couch and slammed her against the back wall. Her drugged look dissipated and she opened her eyes in panic. Her fingers scrabbled at the paneling.

"Please. What's happening? Put me down."

Oh, she'd put her down alright. A snarl on her lips, Ella strode forward, her burning eyes fixated on the object of her ire.

Suddenly, Zane's broad chest blocked her view.

"Ella! You need to stop."

She looked up at him. "Move away from the slut."

"Only if you promise not to hurt her."

A part of Ella understood she was out of control. That she was overreacting. But she couldn't help herself. No one touched Zane. No one but her.

"What does she mean to you?"

One wrong answer, and the woman would die, her soul just another voice she could add to the crowd.

Zane is mine.

Chapter Twenty Two

Confusion initially gripped Zane. When Ella had walked in, he'd thought her fury was a reaction to his feeding, and he couldn't help feeling horrified at being caught in the act. But now, with her words, realization dawned. *She's jealous. Insanely so.*

Zane almost laugh. His earlier fear that she would find his feeding habits disgusting seemed stupid in retrospect. How could he have thought she'd be horrified? She hadn't batted an eye when he'd killed someone for touching her. As for his trepidation she'd be hurt? Closer to the mark. He'd not counted on her jealousy being so violent thought. And sexy.

She tried to step around him, but he wrapped a muscular arm around her, pinning her to his body. Ella didn't struggle, but neither did she relax in his grip. "She means nothing to me, moonbeam. She's just a source of blood. Food. And not even a good meal."

"So you say, but I saw it. She enjoyed your lips on her. Enjoyed you," growled Ella, her usually clear blue eyes almost translucent with power, a power he could feel vibrating through her fragile frame.

"She can't help that. My enzymes make the bite pleasurable for all. Man or woman. It means nothing."

"If you ever feed on me, will it mean

nothing too?"

"No." It emerged more vehemently than expected. "I might not have tasted more than a few drops, but I already know what you and I share transcends anything and anyone else. You are special, moonbeam."

"You say that and yet you left the bed before I woke to hurry off and eat from her."

"Because I hungered and foolishly thought that seeing this side of me would scare you off."

She nose wrinkled. "Scare me why? You're a vampire."

"Exactly and I need to eat."

He could feel the tension easing from her limbs as some of her jealousy receded. "I guess I acted kind of rashly. It's just, after what we shared…"

He understood. After their intimacy, seeing him with another woman must have seemed like a dagger to her fragile heart. He doubted he would have been any better were their roles reversed. "If my feeding from women bothers you, then no more. I will get my sustenance from a man."

Clarity returned to her gaze. "That's just it. I don't want you to feed on anybody else. You're mine."

Her possessiveness pleased him on a primal level. At the same time though, he heard the hurt in her voice. Zane hated the anguish his need for blood had caused her, and would continue to cause. "I wish I didn't have to feed on human blood Ella, but if I don't eat, I will grow weak and die."

Her soft hands came up to cup his face. "I don't want you to stop feeding. I just want you to do it from me. I want to be the one to nourish you."

The breath—what little breath he had in his undead body—left him in a whoosh. His heart swelled and the surge of love, yes love, he felt for this woman made him tremble.

"Even if your spirits don't approve?"

"I don't give a damn what they like," she growled.

"As you wish then. I can go without food for a while. But we'd better get to work on mastering your powers."

"Thank you," she whispered, standing on tiptoe to kiss him. Zane tightened his grasp on her and lifted her so she wouldn't have to crane and returned her fierce embrace.

What he didn't tell was that he wasn't sure if her blood alone would be enough. Zane had always fed from multiple sources. He had to in order to preserve their health and wellbeing. A body could only sustain so much blood loss before it began to shut down. But he'd deal with that problem when they reached it. When Ella trusted him and came to understand she had nothing to fear.

Truth was, the only human he ever wanted to taste again nestled in his arms. Now, they just needed to ensure the spirits didn't kill him when he attempted it.

Chapter Twenty Three

Flopping into a leather chair, Ella groaned. "This isn't working."

Felicia frowned at her. "Something's missing. The power is there, I can sense it. We just need to trigger your control."

"What do you mean by trigger?" asked Zane, who went to stand behind Ella and massaged her tense shoulders.

"Strong emotions would do it. Once she uses the power, then she'll be able to recognize and learn to use it when she's calm. But in the meantime, we need to get her angry or scared."

Ella closed her eyes ignoring Felicia. They'd been at it for over an hour now and the only thing they'd managed was hysterical laughter in her mind as the voices taunted her inability to control them.

Disheartening was putting it mildly. *And I so want to be able to do this. I've got to get control if I ever want to be with Zane or let him feed on me. I don't want him touching anyone else.*

She reached a hand up and lightly stroked the hand at her nape. He leaned down and kissed the top her head. A moment later, his touch disappeared and she heard a grunt. Ella jumped up and saw Felicia held him pinned to the wall, her teeth bared and inches from his throat.

"What are you doing?" exclaimed Ella.

"All this work has made me hungry," said

Felicia with a nonchalant shrug. "You don't mind do you? I've always found Zane to be so *tasty.*"

Rage suffused Ella. "Leave him alone."

"And if I say no?" Felicia smiled at her tauntingly before turning back and moving in for a bite.

A cold wind swirled around Ella, but she barely noticed as she took a step, her hair swirling around her head wildly. "Let. Him. Go," she growled.

Felicia ignored her and bit.

Ella let loose a scream.

Pointing her hands, she grabbed Felicia with ghostly fingers and shook her like a rag doll before tossing her across the room.

Stalking after her, Ella drew in the power she could feel swirling all around her-how could she not have seen it before?-and coalesced it into a giant ball which she pushed with her mind at Felicia.

A thundering crash sounded as her magical blow smashed through the plaster of the office wall into the vacant ballroom beyond.

Familiar arms wrapped around her and she smelled Zane's fresh cologne before he whispered in her ear. "I'm alright. You can calm down now."

Suddenly appalled, yet also secretly exhilarated, she turned and buried her face in Zane's chest. "I'm so sorry," she mumbled against the linen of his shirt. "I killed Felicia."

"Ha, you'd have to try harder than that," scoffed Felicia.

Ella turned around and saw Felicia standing there grinning and uninjured. Brushing the plaster dust off her clothes she said, "I thought that might work."

"You mean you did on purpose?" Ella accused.

"I needed strong emotion," Felicia said, shrugging unapologetically. "Jealousy in this case. Now, did you feel the power that time? I know you manipulated it," she said, smiling ruefully at the large hole in her wall.

"I did. I felt it. But it's gone now."

"That's okay. We've made a start. From here on in, it will get easier. Now if you don't mind, I suddenly find myself famished and since you won't share, I must go for some take-out." Flashing fangs, Felicia left them in the mess of her office.

"You did it, moonbeam," said Zane dropping a kiss on her head. "I knew you could."

But Ella wanted more than a chaste kiss. She yanked his face down and planted a scorcher on his mouth, one that had them both panting and flushed in moments.

"Isn't desire a strong emotion?" she said, smiling at him mischievously.

Zane risked their lives getting them back to his house, his impatience almost as arousing as he was. And when they did finally reach his room…

Oh my. Even she wasn't crazy enough to imagine how good it could be.

Chapter Twenty Four

The car ride back to his home seemed interminable, especially since he could smell the desire radiating from her. See the passion which flickered in her eyes. He was dying for a taste. Whipping around corners and only using his brakes the bare minimum possible, Zane couldn't get them to his bed fast enough.

Her display of jealousy and power might have turned most men off, but Zane found her strength exciting. Just another fascinating aspect to a beautifully complex woman.

Now if only she could direct that power into containing her ghostly friends long enough for him to finally claim her body and make her his.

He screeched to a halt in front of the mansion. Barely acknowledged Hendricks letting them in. Sweeping her into his arms, he practically flew up the stairs to his room and had only just slammed the door shut when his lips claimed hers in a scorching kiss.

Frantic with need, hers as great as his, their hands tore at each other's clothing, buttons popping in their frenzy. Her mouth clung to his hotly and her passionate moans and erratic caresses as she tried to touch him all over at once, fired his blood and made him swell hard enough to burst.

He toppled them onto the bed, skin to skin, her heat a complement to his coolness. Her legs parted to allow him to settle himself between them. Her fingers dug into his scalp as she pressed her lips hard against his, her mouth open so that her tongue could dance wetly along his.

Oh, but he wanted more than just kisses and sinuous body rubbing. Tearing his mouth from hers, he licked his way down her neck, not even pausing at the vein that throbbed so temptingly. He latched instead onto a pink nipple, her cry of delight making his cock jerk impatiently. He sucked the taut peak, drawing it into his mouth, dragging the points of his teeth over her succulent flesh. She delighted in his erotic touch, her cries urging him on, her body bucking underneath him, silently begging for more.

Her breasts quivered under his oral onslaught, the nubs tight as he nibbled them one after another. He let his hand drift down to quest between her legs, her moist juices making him thirsty for something other than blood. Eager to taste her again, he slid down her body, his mouth seeking and finding her molten core.

Lapping at her with his tongue, he devoured her sweet nectar, his hands holding her down even as she bucked and thrashed. When her first orgasm hit, he slid his finger into her tight sheath almost coming at the exquisite feel of her muscles clenching around his digit.

Applying his tongue again to her clit, he built up her pleasure again, bringing her back to the brink.

Ella moaned a, "Please," that he could not ignore. He slid up her body, the thick head of his cock nudging her moist entrance.

A part of him wanted to plunge into her

velvety wetness without further ado. Forget more foreplay. Forget everything, even the danger to him if the ghosts got mad. If he didn't claim her, he might go mad himself. He'd reached the point of no return. Whether she could control the souls or not, he'd fuck her tonight. Claim her body and heart as his. He could wait no longer and would suffer the painful consequences if need be. Anything to feel her orgasm as he nestled deep within her.

A cool breeze blew through the room, but the souls didn't assault him. It probably helped he'd had loose objects removed ahead of time, a preparation just in case Ella's lessons were successful. Frustrated, the spirits pulled at him with ghostly fingers.

"Ella," he murmured, refusing to budge.

Opening passion glazed eyes that shone with power, he felt rather than saw her push away the souls that would prevent their joining.

"Love me, Zane," she whispered.

"Forever," he replied and he thrust into her.

The hands that stroked his back clawed him for a moment as he breached her maidenhead and a chill wind blew across his now feverish skin. Zane held his position for a moment, trying to not breathe too deeply, the scent of the blood—the pure blood of her virginity—surrounding him. Slowly, he moved inside her, her exquisite tightness almost making him come. Reining in his desire to pound at her flesh and shoot his cream, he stroked her slowly, allowing her to get used to his size.

Soon, she forgot the pain of his entry and she clung to him in passion again. Her hips found his rhythm and matched it.

Increasing his pace, he leaned down and flicked her nipple with his tongue. Faster, he thrust, her whimpering cries building in intensity until with a drawn out scream, she orgasmed around his cock, the tightness of her sex making him bellow in return as he came inside of her, marking her forever more as his.

Shaken by the intensity of their lovemaking, he stared down at her. *There is no denying it. I, a three hundred plus year old vampire, have fallen in love.*

Chapter Twenty Five

Marcus sat lotus style, utterly naked, in a circle of tallow candles—made from only the purest of human fat-his lean body gleaming with sweat as he chanted. Eyes shut, he recited by memory alone the words to the spell which forced the souls he'd harnessed to obey him. It irked him each time he had to use them. The bitch who'd escaped didn't have to recite mumbo jumbo and degrade herself to achieve power, it came to her naturally.

But not for much longer.

To think, he'd not even known such a thing as harnessing souls was possible until a few years ago. In a dusty grimoire, encased in a strange leather cover, he came across a whole chapter dedicated to describing the abilities of an *ánima veneficus*. Soul sorcerers. How he coveted such a power, especially once he learned from his book of black magic that such a skill could be stolen with the right spell, a spell which the book handily provided. If cast successfully, a person became more than just a spellcaster but a force to be reckoned with. Someone who made the rules and whom people would obey. Out of fear or might, he didn't care which.

All he needed was to find someone with the talent to attract the dead, and steal their ability. Someone like Ella. He'd spent years seeking out *ánima veneficus*. Testing countless mental patients who claimed to hear voices. Most were just crazy. But some suffered from the power he coveted; the ability to attract and control the dead. Of course, they didn't realize that. They believed society when told they weren't normal. They languished and decayed in hospitals until he came along and set them free. The powers he stole from them, though, were weak. Too weak to give him the grandeur he aspired to. He'd almost given up hope when he came across Ella. The girl fairly radiated power. The etheric forces swirling about her almost visible, especially to someone like him in touch with the other side. It made him fairly drool to think of all that power, his for the taking. Once he found her that was.

It made the acidic rage in his stomach boil anew whenever he thought of how close he'd come only to have her slip through his grip. He'd pulled so many strings getting her transferred to his hospital. Greased so many palms. To have her vanish, just when he'd been preparing himself to siphon her, galled him to the extreme.

But he'd get her back.

Lost for the moment, he'd found a way to find her. The grimoire had a method for him to locate the missing girl, and once he had her back in his control, he'd cast the spell to siphon her power. Then, with the magic that he'd have at his fingertips, the council of wizards would bow to him…and he could rule them all.

First though, he needed to get his hands on Ella.

Sweat poured off him as he continued to chant and follow the ritual steps of the spell designed to give him control over the spirits that resided in the ether around him. At the peak of the spell, using a dagger inscribed with runes, he cut himself and dripped his blood onto the black candle that burned in the center of his drawn circle.

Souls, drawn unwilling and wailing, entered the room and spun, creating a vortex of moans and shadows.

He ignored them, used by now to their bitching. Holding tight to the gathered energy, his strength waning fast, Marcus croaked out the question.

"Where is the girl? Where is Ella?"

Forced to do his bidding, the ghosts caught in limbo showed him where she could be found, and Marcus cackled even as he released the powerful binding that sapped him.

I've got you now, bitch.

Chapter Twenty Six

"I love you." He whispered the words, and Ella's breath stopped. Surely she'd misunderstood. Perhaps her mind, or her ghostly companions, played tricks on her. She opened her eyes and saw Zane gazing down at her intently.

"What did you say?"

"I love you, moonbeam."

No mistake. Tears brimmed in her eyes and her lips trembled. She wanted to speak. To tell him she loved him too, but her throat closed tight even though she'd craved this moment all her life.

Tender fingers wiped at the moisture which leaked. "Don't cry. I know you've been hurt all your life and lonely. Never again, this I promise you."

Ella still couldn't speak, but she smiled tremulously and nodded her head.

"That's my sweet moonbeam. Come. Let me bathe the blood off you before I treat you like dinner."

Ella giggled at his poor excuse of a joke, a laughter that turned into a squeal when he swept her into his arms and carried her into his bathroom.

He ran the water with her snuggled on his lap. Ella could have stayed cuddled in his arms forever. She hugged him, her cheek pressed against his chest. It seemed like a dream. A fairy tale come true. She couldn't believe how lucky she'd suddenly gotten.

A luck that improved even more when he climbed into the bath with her and with dexterous fingers bathed her.

Ella leaned back against him, smiling when his cock, already hard again, nudged her backside. The voices had stayed quiet since she'd pushed them away in the bedroom. And if they knew what was good for them, they'd stay that way. She was done letting them push her around. From now on, she'd call the shots. She would control her life and destiny. Control her future, a future which held Zane. *My vampire lover.*

Soapy fingers rubbed at her breasts and Ella watched in erotic fascination as Zane tweaked her nipples until they both pointed proudly from her chest. Slowly, he slid his hand down her stomach into the water, finding and lightly stroking her. Ella's breath hitched as he rubbed her clit, stoking the fire that hadn't left her body since she'd met him.

"Get on your knees and grab the edge of the tub," he ordered.

She didn't argue. She trusted him. She knew he wouldn't hurt her. On the contrary, she looked forward to the pleasure his eyes promised. Her hands gripped the cold edge of the tub as she knelt on her knees which had the effect of putting her bottom almost in his face, right where he wanted her.

Clasping each of her cheeks with a hand, he buried his face and Ella shuddered in anticipation. He spread her wide and licked her from her tight puckered hole to her sensitized clit.

"Oh, do that again," she moaned.

Slowly, he lapped her again, front to back,

then back to front. Ella clutched the side of the tub desperately.

"Do you like it when I lick you?" he asked gruffly putting action to his words.

Shivering, Ella replied. "Yes. Oh, yes."

Grunting in satisfaction at her words, he delved between her wet folds, nuzzling her sex.

With an oath, he pulled away and Ella looked over her shoulder at him.

"Please don't stop."

"I can still smell the blood of your breaching. I dare not taste you until you heal, else I might not control myself."

"Then bite me," she said, wiggling her bottom at him. "I told you that I wanted to be the one to feed you and I meant it. I love you." She said the words finally, the fierce look of joy on his face jolting her in a pleasurable way.

With no further encouragement, his mouth sucked at the plump lips of her sex, his tongue spreading her and stabbing inside. His fingers dug into her buttocks as he kept her positioned for his enjoyment. Pleasure coiled inside her, her womb tightening and readying itself to come again.

Taking his mouth off her sex, she made a sound of protest which transitioned into a mewl of pleasure as he replaced it with two probing fingers. He stroked her wet channel as his lips brushed the tender skin of her thigh.

Then he bit her and Ella, who'd already seen heaven once, saw it again, this time with fireworks.

Chapter Twenty Seven

Zane sank his teeth into her willing flesh, and immediately she came, keening his name, her pelvic muscles spasming around his fingers. He couldn't help but close his eyes and groan at the ecstasy, her blood unlike anything he'd ever tasted.

In the back of his mind, Zane vaguely realized he'd shot his own load of come, so intense was the rapture that went through him at the ambrosia running through her veins. Unlike the small taste he'd gotten previously, this was a thick, undiluted meal, and it went beyond pleasurable right into fucking amazing, mind blowing and even those words didn't come close to explaining how it felt.

He also found he didn't need as much for strength to course through him, energizing him like he'd never imagined. Mindful of the fact she was human, and couldn't handle giving him too much, he released her skin with reluctance, a swipe of his tongue halting the blood flow.

She barely reacted, other than to moan his name.

Wrapping his drowsy moonbeam first in a towel, he then carried her back to bed and tucked her in. Dawn was still an hour or so away and the blood he'd ingested made him too restless to sleep yet.

"I'm going to work in my office for a bit," he murmured as he kissed her swollen lips.

"Love you," she whispered with eyes already shut.

"I love you too, moonbeam. I'll see you when the sun sets."

Leaving her sleeping, he went down to his office, but ran into Hendricks on the way.

"Master, a doctor called earlier this eve and asked to speak to your young lady."

"What?" His words sent a chill of foreboding down Zane's spine.

"He claimed he was Milady's doctor and that he was looking for her. That someone had mentioned she might be staying with you."

Impossible! "You told him nothing?" said Zane sharply.

"Of course, I didn't," said Hendricks indignantly. "But as an added precaution, I've increased the security around the house and grounds."

"Excellent. If Ella wakes before I do on the morrow, keep her close to the house. Perhaps, I'll take her to my villa in Italy for a while. It's been a while since I've visited my estate there."

Actually the more he thought of it, the more he wanted to take Ella to see his other home. Take her away and show her the world and the wonders it had to offer. "On second thought, I will take her tonight. Please see to the preparations."

"A sound idea, Master. I will make arrangements for your departure." With a short bow, Hendricks took his leave.

Restless, Zane pondered on what clue he'd inadvertently left at the institution that had led the human doctor here. He could think of nothing, and that worried him.

    I will not allow this doctor to take my moonbeam. I'll kill him first. Or eat him. A smart vampire never let blood go to waste.

Chapter Twenty Eight

The body slumped to the ground and Marcus uttered a disdainful sniff. Too easy. He'd dispatched the man with just one blow to the head. He'd expected better security from a vampire. Make that less human security now. If this was all the man had then his objective—reclaim Ella-would be easier than he'd expected. But just in case the vamp proved stronger than his magic, he needed to move faster because the sun had begun to dip.

He'd meant to arrive earlier when the sun still sat high in the sky, however a string of incidents from a flat tire, to a construction detour and more led to him arriving later than scheduled. He debated for a moment, coming back the next day, bright and early. The problem with leaving now was the string of dead guards he'd left in his wake as he scouted the grounds. Their bodies would act as a glaring warning that someone invaded the vampire's premises. The last thing Marcus wanted was for the vampire to get spooked and run. With the kind of funds this bloodsucker appeared to have at his disposal, he could have her out of the country in a heartbeat.

Fuck it. He'd come here to get Ella and he wasn't leaving until he had her in his grasp. He'd just have to move faster, snag the stupid girl and be gone before the sun set.

Inching closer and closer to the house, he

couldn't believe his dumb luck when Ella of all people came out of some French doors at the back of the house cradling a steaming cup.

He practically drooled as he imagined the power he'd soon claim as his own.

Chapter Twenty Nine

"Hello, Ella."

She almost dropped her cup of coffee when Dr. Peters came strolling nonchalantly through the hedges that bordered the patio and pool. How had he found her?

"Dr. P-Peters," she stuttered in shock. "What are you doing here?"

"Why, I've come to take you back of course, Ella. You didn't really think we'd just let you walk away did you?" he said smiling even as he kept approaching.

The voices hissed in her mind.

"Bad man. He wants to hurt you."

"Quick. Someone wake the vamp."

"Run foolish girl."

Ella cocked her head as she listened to what the voices had to say. Straightening her spine, she regarded the doctor coldly. "Stop where you are."

"Why? I won't hurt you. You know I just want to help you."

"I don't need help. Not anymore."

"Now, now, Ella. We both know that's not true. A girl like you needs the safety of the institution. You wouldn't want to accidentally hurt yourself or others. Come with me and I promise you won't be punished for running."

"Liar. Did you forget?" She smiled at him, a knowing smile that made him falter. "I hear voices, and they don't like you."

"Smart spirits," replied the doctor just before he threw something at her face, something liquid which burned and made her drop to her knees with a cry.

Wrenching hands pulled her arms behind her back and bound them.

"There's no use calling out. The sun hasn't quite set yet and I've taken care of the staff," taunted Dr. Peters.

Ella cried out anyway. "Zane!"

Dr. Peters slapped her across the face, the edge of a ring cutting her lip. Ella could taste the blood in her mouth, and it hurt, but she could also sense her power coiling as she and her little friends upstairs got mad. "Shut up. There's no help for you."

"You shouldn't have done that," she said in a low voice, pulling in more of the power, the voices cheering and babbling in her mind. Her hair fluttered and the potted plants lining the patio lifted in the air, and hovered menacingly.

The doctor smirked. "I see someone's had some lessons since she escaped."

"I know that I'm not crazy. And I'm warning you right now, if you don't leave, you will regret it."

"You wouldn't dare. I know you, Ella. You're too good to hurt others. Too soft," he mocked.

"That's what you think." One of the vases heaved itself and shattered at his feet, startling him enough that he flinched.

For a moment, she thought she'd won, but

with a chilling smile, Dr. Peters pulled out a lighter and flicked it. The flame burned steadily and as she watched, almost hypnotized, as the doctor dug into the pocket of his trench coat and pulled out a bottle with a rag stuck in it.

"What are you doing?" she asked nervously, a sickening dread in her stomach.

"Fight me and this Molotov cocktail gets lit and thrown in the house," he said, tilting his head towards the open patio door. "What do you think will kill your vampire friend first? Smoke inhalation? Or will he burn to death?"

Instantly, all the hovering missiles hit the ground with a crash. She couldn't let Dr. Peters carry through with his threat. Zane slept. He'd die, and that was the one thing she couldn't allow. Not if she could stop it. "No, don't." Ella couldn't help her beseeching plea. "I'll go with you, just put the fire out."

Dr. Peters smiled in triumph.

"Step away from him, Ella. You're not going anywhere," boomed Zane's voice as he stood in the shadow of the door.

Chapter Thirty

Zane wanted to bellow and curse at the predicament they found themselves in. Even in his deathlike slumber, he'd heard Ella's cry for help. Despite the fact the sun still sat high in the sky, he'd woken instantly. He had to. Ella—*my Ella*—was in danger.

Practically flying, he'd ran down the stairs, instinct guiding him to the rear patio, only to find himself enveloped in frustration. A bystander to the unfolding drama, he burned with helpless anger because the menace threatening his moonbeam lay out of his reach, smack dab in the deadly rays of sunlight.

Despite the danger, he tried to take a step forward. Burning pain sizzled through his body and his exposed skin smoked.

"Zane, no!" Ella cried.

Hissing Zane took a step back, cursing his impotence.

The man, whom Zane assumed to be the doctor who'd called seeking Ella previously, smiled nastily. "Don't worry. I'll take good care of Ella." He used one hand to pat her on the head where she knelt, hands bound with tape behind her back. Foolish girl instead of looking scared, her face twisted with ire, an expression that turned into rage when the puny man lit his makeshift bomb and threw it at the house.

Zane wasn't stupid. He knew what a Molotov cocktail when he saw one. He let the flaming bottle crash over his head, not crazy enough to catch the glass that would explode. He called out to Hendricks whom he sensed entering the room, out of breath as if he'd run. "Get the extinguisher." *Because I'm going after Ella, daylight or not.*

But in the seconds he'd been distracted Ella had taken matters into her own hands—ghostly ones.

Screaming in rage, she stood. The tethers, which had bound her, fell to her feet in a sift of ash. Lifted by a ghostly wind, her hair floated in a halo around her head. Even more amazing, she floated a few inches off the ground.

Zane's heart almost burst with love and his cock with lust, as his moonbeam, energized by her soul companions and looking like an absolute goddess of vengeance, saved herself. Power swirled about her, the esoteric forces so strong he could practically see them. They coalesced and did her bidding. Ella raised her hands, and up went the doctor, the magic she controlled holding the bastard above ground despite his kicking and screaming.

"How." She took a step towards the doctor, her eyes glowing an almost translucent blue. "Dare." Another step. "You try to hurt Zane!" she shouted.

A flick of her hands and the doctor flew backwards. He hit the wall beside the door with a crash. Snaking an arm out and swallowing at the burning pain, Zane snagged the limp form of the one who dared threaten *his* woman and dragged him into the shadows of the house.

He held the bastard off the ground. "You

shouldn't have touched her," he said with a snarl before he snapped his neck and tossed him to the side.

Then he held his arms open in time for the woman he'd come to love to hurtle herself into them. His moonbeam was safe.

Chapter Thirty One

In the soothing comfort of Zane's arms, Ella's rage and fear subsided. When she'd seen the doctor throw the bomb, she'd lost her mind. Not an unusual occurrence for her in the past, but this time, she controlled the outcome.

I protected myself and took care of him. She just didn't quite understand why Dr. Peters had acted like he did. Nor did she really care. He was dead. Zane was safe. Nothing else mattered.

Tilting her head, she asked for reassurance, and he gave it in the form of kiss, swallowing her shuddering sigh of relief.

His hands roamed her body. "Are you injured?" he murmured in between nibbles.

"No," she whispered back before sucking on his lower lip. "You?"

"Already healing."

"What about the bomb?"

"Hendricks took care of it."

The sound of rending cloth preceded the cool air on her bared buttocks. "What are you doing?" she gasped, as he kneaded her nude flesh.

"I need you. Now," he said picking her up. "Put your legs around my waist."

Ella eagerly complied, the throbbing hardness of his cock pulsing against her moist sex.

A wall braced her back, as Zane, his lips still devouring hers, pushed her up against the nearest one.

His big, capable hands cupped her buttocks and rubbed his erection against her sex, driving her wild.

"Stop teasing, Zane," she moaned, her tone impatient, her breathing ragged.

"Or?" he queried as he ground himself against her.

"Or I'll use my new powers to hold you down helpless while I torture you."

Zane groaned. "That's not a threat. Promise me you'll try it later."

She laughed, then gasped as the mushroomed head of his cock probed at her plump lips. When he slid inside, Ella sighed. Deeper he went, his thickness stretching her pleasantly and she clenched around him.

Still holding her with an arousing strength, he pumped her, his rod slipping in and out of her tight sheath, hitting the bottom of her womb and making her cry out.

Faster he drilled her. The pleasure built in her body, a coiling heat that made her clutch at his shoulders tightly.

"Bite me?" she asked.

"With pleasure." He buried his face in the curve of her neck, his hips still pistoning and when his sharp teeth broke her skin, Ella screamed.

Wave after wave of bliss rolled through her body, a never ending rapture that left her floating.

With a shudder, she vaguely felt Zane's body go rigid as he spilled inside of her, his own pleasure found.

Arms wrapped tightly around her, he

nuzzled her cheek and whispered. "I love you."

"And I'm *crazy* about you," she murmured back.

She joined him in laughter, cherishing the moment and the love she'd found.

And the voices smartly said nothing to ruin it.

Epilogue

Zane left his beloved moonbeam in the care of Felicia, the person he trusted most besides him to have the power to keep Ella safe. Oddly enough, his moonbeam and oldest vampire friend had hit it off and not just because of the magic. Felicia said she found Ella refreshing.

It was just as well they'd decided to do a marathon of Blade movies for he had other business to attend to. Hendricks had dug up the information Zane had requested and now he stood in front of a small, well-kept home.

Unlike the movies and the legends, he didn't need an invitation to enter and puny locks did not hinder him. His night vision helped him navigate the cluttered home until he stood over the sleeping occupant. How benign the gray haired matron seemed. But he knew better. Ella's mother was anything but gentle and kind. Only the coldest of bitches would sentence an innocent child to a lifetime of misery because she happened to be different.

Ella claimed she didn't care and that she understood why her parents abandoned her. Zane however knew better. He'd seen the hurt Ella tried to hide when she'd finally told him about her childhood.

An eye for an eye he always said. This pathetic excuse of a woman had hurt his moonbeam, and now he would hurt her in return. The father had unfortunately passed away many years before else he'd also be facing Zane's brand of justice.

In seconds, he held the cow by the throat, pinned to the wall. Her eyes opened and bulged as she gasped for air.

"Well, if it isn't the mother of the year," he drawled sarcastically. "I'm here on Ella's behalf."

The older woman made choking sounds and Zane let up the pressure on her just enough to let her speak.

"Did you have something to say? Maybe how it was cruel to dump your daughter at the asylum and never look back. She was just a little girl," he snarled.

"She's—She's not my daughter."

The words made his eyes widen in surprise then narrow. He took his hand off her throat and let her feet drop to the floor. She staggered and rubbed at her neck.

"Explain," he said, crossing his arms over his chest intimidatingly.

Babbling quickly she told him the short tale. In a nutshell, she and her husband were unable to have children of their own. One day, they woke to find on their kitchen table a basket with a sleeping baby girl. Documents attesting they were the parents plus a sum of money had been left with the baby along with a cryptic note.

"Do you still have the note?" he asked, baffled at this strange turn of events.

The woman licked her dry lips. "No, but I remember what it said. 'Guard her well for the fate of humanity may rest on her.'"

The message sent a chill through Zane. What did it mean? He'd ponder it later. He still had unfinished business to attend to. "You didn't do a very good job of guarding though, did you?" he accused.

"You don't know what it was like. Even as a baby, she was strange. As she got older, it got worse. She could hear voices and the things she claimed they told her. Disgusting."

"So you had her locked up?"

"We did it for her own good. Don't you see? We had to." The woman defended her actions.

But Zane hadn't heard anything that justified their vile act. He tried her in the court of his morality and found her... guilty.

So he killed her. Welcome to his version of justice.

*

Ella sensed Zane the moment he stepped into Felicia's office and she turned to face him with a smile. As always, when she saw him, even looking so fierce, her heart skipped a beat. *So handsome and all mine.*

It still amazed her that someone like him could love her. *But then again, I'm not the girl I used to be or thought I was.*

Drastic was the only word to describe all the major changes in her life. Discovering she had an innate power and even better, learning how to use that ability, removed her last traces of fear. *Now let them try and lock me away. With my newfound powers, I will never be a prisoner again.*

Ella wondered at the grim look Zane wore as he strode to her, but she forgot everything as usual when he swept her into his arms and kissed her hard. The flames of her desire ignited immediately and she thanked providence when she sensed Felicia, who had been teaching her in his absence, left the room.

But before she allowed the distraction of his lips and her lust to make her forget…she pulled her lips reluctantly from his. "I want to show you something."

"That's funny, so do I." He gave her such a masculine grin of pure mischief, she melted, heat pooling between her legs.

"Zane, please. I've been practicing all night."

"What happened to watching movies?" He cocked a brow at her, but she could tell he wasn't angry.

Ella stepped back from him and closed her eyes. She concentrated and directed what she wanted the energy to do. Slowly, her feet left the floor as she hovered in the air. She opened her eyes and smiled triumphantly at him. "I can float. Now the next time we need to scale a wall, I'll be able to do it myself!"

*

Zane chuckled at her obvious pleasure in her new ability. "I'd prefer to carry you personally, maybe naked next time if you don't mind, but I'm happy you're learning to use your powers."

As he hugged her tight, he closed his eyes

and buried his face in her silvery hair, enjoying the warmth of her presence. He also made a decision.

He'd debated on the ride back from Ella's mother what he would do or say about what he'd learned. Honestly, the fate of the world bothered him not one bit, but Ella's did. Forewarned, vigilance would be his new mandate, always alert to possible danger, ready to protect her. *I will let no one, be they man, beast or spirit, harm you my precious moonbeam. You and I shall be together…forever.*

The End…or is it?

If you enjoyed this story, then I invite you to check out more of my books at EveLanglais.com